Hearts That Heal

Genevieve Lollar

contents

CHAPTER 1

Some days it's easier to get out of bed, the sun is shining and for the first twenty minutes of the day I can pretend that everything is alright. Today was not one of those days.

My head was pounding when I walked into my bathroom, my hand running along the wall as I looked for the light switch. I flicked it on when I found it, wincing once the light illuminated the room; my reaction was partly because of how much the light hurt my eyes and partly because of the face looking back at me in the mirror.

I ran a hand through my knotted hair, praying that the ripping sounds that I heard didn't permanently damage my hair. My brown hair fell flat against the side of my face when I was done removing all of the knots, leaving me to deal with the rest of my face. The purple bags under my eyes seem to be getting darker and darker as each day passed, even when I put concealer on they still made an appearance.

My mum poked her head through the bathroom door just as I finished throwing my hair up into a messy bun, she seemed hesitant to speak- which was normal with anyone around me nowadays.

I met her eyes in the mirror and raised my eyebrows expectantly; I waited for her to say whatever she had to say. Mum sighed and ran a hand across her forehead before she said, "you're going to be late."

I hit the 'on' button on my phone and quickly checked the time, "I have another ten minutes."

She shook her head, her hair covering her eyes before she tucked it behind her ears. I took a moment to study her face as she collected her thoughts. In the past couple of months I had seen multiple new wrinkles appear on her face, making her look nearly ten years older. Her blue eyes, which I had inherited from her, seemed to have changed to a dull gray colour.

"You need to eat." She finally spoke, emphasizing her words. It was obvious that she wouldn't let me walk out of this house without some sort of food in my body.

But I sure as hell was going to try anyways. "I'm not hungry."

"Zoe."

"Mum."

"Don't do this to me, not now. It's your first day of school without-" she stopped herself short. Her eyes dropped to the floor, refusing to meet my glare.

"Without Mark? You think I don't know that?"

She ran her hand across her forehead again and for a split second I felt almost sympathetic. Almost.

"I'm going to go to school now." I squeezed by her and out into the hallway, trying not to notice the pained expression on her face as I did so. I knew that she had already lost one child and she didn't want to lose the other, but I couldn't help but feeling that she had already lost us both.

I nervously tapped my fingers on the steering wheel of the old beat up black Toyota that I was driving, watching as students walked towards the front doors. Some ran up to each other; the boys high fiving and the girls hugging, they all acted like they hadn't seen each other in years.

I leaned back in my seat, my nervous fingers moving from my steering wheel to the straps of my backpack- I picked at a loose thread as I worked up the nerve to get out of my car.

Then I saw what I had been waiting for. I held my breath as I saw my former best friend walk towards the school. Elli had barely changed since I last saw her nearly two months ago, at Mark's funeral. She had cut her hair shoulder length but that didn't surprise me since she changed her hair drastically twice every year, saying that it symbolized her ever changing personality as she so eloquently told me on multiple occasions.

What did surprise me though, was Henry Jones- who walked up to Elli and stopped her on her way into the school, giving her a kiss before they continued the walk together. I wanted to be happy for her; Elli had a crush on Henry for almost as long as I've had a crush on Carter Jacobs, yet I had this nagging thought of why are they able to move on so easily and I'm not?

I closed my eyes and took a deep breath while I tried to calm myself down. When I opened my eyes again, they're gone and I quickly grabbed my bag and hopped out of the car. I walked towards the school before I could change my mind.

Last year at this same time I was walking through the school with my head held high and my brother's arm around my shoulder.

"This is going to be our year." Mark had informed me, highfiving a few people as we passed them.

"Our year?" I questioned and I tried not to laugh, knowing that Mark was having one of his 'the future is now' moments.

"Yeah," He turned his attention toward me, a full blown smile on his face, "our year."

"What do you mean?"

Mark shrugged, his blonde hair falling over his eyes. That was the only way that we were different; the colour of our hair. We had the same matching blue eyes and the same soft facial structure. "I have a feeling that something big is going to happen."

"Like what?" I inquired while simultaneously wondering what it would be like to be inside of his head. From out here, it looked like a very scary place.

He shrugged again; his attention was already leaving me and instead focusing on our large group of friends that were sauntering down the hallway towards us. His gaze flickered back to me for a second, "I guess we'll have to just wait and see." Then he was gone, leaving me and walking off towards our friends at the end of the hallway.

My first period math class was empty when I walked in. I breathed a sigh of relief and quickly picked a seat in the back row nearest the windows.

"Oh!" My head flew up when I heard the noise, thinking it was one of my friends. Luckily, it was just the math teacher; Mrs. Abrams. Her hand was resting over her mouth as she took in my slumped form. "You startled me, darling. What are you doing here so early? There's still another ten minutes before class starts."

I twisted my lips, focusing on my binder on the desk. I played with the corners that had started to fray from being shoved force-fully into the locker one too many times. I hadn't been in the mood to do any back to school shopping, other than Mom buying me a new pack of pencils I was using everything from last year.

"I had nothing better to do." I stated flatly, my eyes not leaving the desk.

"Well," she started; pausing for a second as she placed her briefcase and papers on the desk in front of her, "you're more than welcome to come to class early whenever you'd like."

I didn't answer her; instead I focused on the ticking clock hanging next to the door. With every passing second the knot in my stomach seemed to grow larger and larger. Until finally, two minutes before the bell was set to ring, the other students started walking in. I let the loose strands of hair from my bun fall over my face, praying that no one would notice me sitting back here.

My prayers were nearly answered when the bell rang and the seat next to me remained vacant. That was until the door flew open and in walked Elli; the one person that I used to call my best friend. I looked towards the window, hoping that she would find a seat at the front of the class room- where all of her friends were sitting.

"Hey, Zoe."

I closed my eyes and practiced the breathing techniques that my therapist had taught me. She had been the one to suggest that I came back to this school, saying that I couldn't stop myself from going somewhere just because it would remind me of Mark. Let me tell you, I hated that lady with such a burning passion it wasn't even funny. And I wasn't afraid to tell her that either.

On top of that I thought that she was crazy for making me come back here, I begged my parents for a solid two weeks not to make me come back to this school. I thought that I had nearly broken their tough facade when they didn't bring up the subject for the week before school started. That was until I woke up one morning to the sight of this year's registration papers lying in front of me. Then I knew that there was no turning back, they had made up their minds.

I didn't respond to Elli, keeping my eyes trained on Mrs. Abrams instead as she welcomed us to back to school for our senior year.

The class seemed to drag on, Elli kept trying to start a conversation with me but I tried my hardest to tune her out. She was just another reminder of my brother that I didn't need.

Nearly thirty seconds before the bell rang Elli turned her body towards me; her eyes were narrowed as she took me in. I knew this look. This was Elli's 'take no prisoners' look; she was ready to say what was really on her mind. "You look like crap."

I grunted, if Elli thought that telling me how bad I looked would get me to talk to her she had another thing coming to her.

She took my reaction as some form of encouragement and said, "You can't push everyone away. We want to help you." Elli placed her hand on top of mine, "We're still you're friends."

"I can do whatever the hell I want, Elli."

Before she had a chance to respond, the bell rang; giving me the perfect opportunity to escape. I pulled my hand away and gathered up my stuff before I practically sprinted out of the room, not giving Elli a chance to catch up.

It wouldn't be until the last class of the day that I bumped into my old group of friends. I had managed to avoid them during my other classes, making sure that the seat next to me was filled before they had a chance to ambush me. It wasn't that hard, they were always the last ones to class so making sure that they didn't sit next to me wasn't exactly impossible.

Unfortunately my plan to avoid them had a kink thrown in it when my science teacher held me back after class to tell me that how sorry he was for my loss, and how much he had loved having my brother as a student. I had tried my hardest not to cry but the tears inevitably started rolling as the door to the science lab shut behind me. I made a quick trip to the bathroom to fix my makeup, not wanting to walk into English class with mascara streaks running down my face. This resulted in me being ten minutes late to my last class.

I hesitated with my hand on the door knob to my English class, I thought about just leaving and going home. Maybe trying again tomorrow, but I knew that my parent's would be none too pleased, and we already weren't on good terms, so with a shaking hand I pushed open the door.

"Nice of you to joi-"My teacher stopped his talking when he raised his head and saw me standing there. "Oh, Zoe. Would you to take a seat over there next to-" he stopped and quickly checked his attendance list, "Carter Jacobs."

My breathing stopped for a minute when Carter raised his gaze to meet mine. I was tempted to smile until I remembered all of the times when I needed him over the past couple of months and he was nowhere to be found. So I quickly turned back to Mr. Smith before I got sucked into his gaze. "Is there anywhere else that I could sit?" I knew that there were no empty desks left, but I was hoping for some sort of miracle.

I could feel Carter looking at me, his face was probably ex-pressionless. I always used to think that he practiced that look in the bathroom mirror but over the years I had come to learn that was just Carter. The same way he had those perfect white teeth, tanned skin, gorgeous green eyes and dirty blonde hair- the whole surfer boy look was just Carter. He didn't whiten his teeth, he didn't spend time tanning on the beach and he only brushed his hair when he really wanted to. It all seemed to come naturally to him.

"Unfortunately there are no more available seats, Miss. Finley." Mr. Smith rested his hands on the desk and looked at me over the top of his glasses. His gaze shifted from me to the class,

"Unless anyone is willing to switch spots and sit next to Mr. Jacobs instead?"

No one was going to raise their hands, I knew that they wouldn't. Carter was giving off an air of indifference and everyone- as much as they'd love to sit next to infamous Carter- wouldn't dare risk getting on his bad side.

"Sorry Zoe, now if you don't mind taking a seat so that we can get this class started." Mr. Smith turned his back to me and began writing on the chalk board. That was it, the conversation was over. My mind was running with how I could possibly get myself out of this situation, but I saw no possible escape plan except to suffer through this class and hopefully get here early enough tomorrow to get another seat.

I felt defeated as I walked over to sit next to Carter; I threw my binders on to the desk and pulled out the chair. It felt like the simple motion took all the energy left in my body, my shoulders slumped as I collapsed into my seat and listened to Mr. Smith start telling us about the course syllabus.

I tensed when I felt Carter move and lean forward a little bit. "Don't talk to me." I snapped, my gaze not leaving the board. I knew he had probably talked to Elli at lunch and come up with this grand plan to get me back to being my old self.

"I wasn't going to." Carter snapped back, his pencil scribbling down what Mr. Smith had begun writing.

I bit my lip, trying not to cry. I couldn't handle this. Not Carter, not Elli. Not the ghost of Mark that I saw in every corner of the hallway. I couldn't do this.

I closed my binder and stood up quickly, my chair made a loud clanging noise when it hit the desk behind me. "Mr. Smith, I-"I took a deep breath. Practice your breathing exercises, I told myself; don't cry until you're out in the hallway. "I have to go."

I practically flew out of the classroom. I knew that everyone was looking at me, probably with that stupid sympathetic gaze that made wish that I had been the one to die, but I didn't care. All that I cared about was getting as far away from that school as I possibly could.

CHAPTER 2

When I was fourteen, I had this slight obsession with YouTube. YouTube is a video sharing website, where people posted clips of anything from people falling on black ice to videos of them singing.

I spent three days trying to pick my username. There were some really creative ones out there, a creativity level that I couldn't possibly match. So, I pulled out a notebook and filled three pages -back and front- with username ideas. I finally settled on Simply-Zoe.

I wanted my first video to be something original, not a cover of an overplayed song or anything along those lines. So my first post was something unique, something that had 'Zoe Finley' written all over it.

It's funny; I had all these ideas for what my first video would be. Maybe I would sit down and do one of those '50 Things about Me' tags, or maybe I would show off my best painting. This, at that time, was nothing more than a painting of our house with a rainbow in the distance. To be honest, a five year old could have painted something much better.

Mine and my brother's fourteenth birthday had rolled around while I was in the process of choosing my first video, and for the birthday party I had decided to have a pool party. Everyone was doing it, and at that age I would do whatever was considered cool at the time.

Mark had told me that he was going to have his own birthday party at the local arcade rather than share the party with me. So I wasn't surprised when I go up the morning of my birthday party and saw a card from my brother lying on the kitchen table along with a note saying that he would see me later that night.

I was surprised however when I felt two strong hands pick me up and throw me in the pool; and never in a million years did I expect it to be my brother. But it was him; he told me that he had been planning this since I first picked a date for my party since he thought that him and I sharing our party was better than any present he could get me. Of course he told me this after I had gotten out of the pool with my white t-shirt nearly see-through.

My first video ended up being a mistake, nothing that I could have ever planned out. Mum had a camera rolling and caught Mark's surprise on film. Two days after my birthday party, I uploaded it. The video went viral, gaining 100,000 views within the first twenty-four hours. I think it was my screams that gathered all of the popularity.

I took the video off of YouTube on the day of Mark's funeral, wanting to keep the moment for myself. Even though nearly two million people had already seen it, I didn't want any more too.

It's funny really, because I haven't watched the video since he died.

I used to hate books. I hated the smell; I hated the words upon words that would blur together when I looked at them for too long, I hated every single aspect of books. The only type of book that I would consider touching would be textbooks and that was only when my parent's threatened to take away my car if I didn't pass my next test, therefore meaning that I actually had to study.

My brother, on the other hand, spent the majority of his free time wrapped up in one fictional story after the other. His room was littered with books, shoved into every nook and cranny. It was Mark's guilty pleasure that only myself and my parents knew about.

Shortly after my brother died I found a book underneath my bed with a note written in the front cover. It had read;

To Zo,

Maybe this will be the one that changes your opinion? Happy birthday sis,

Mark

I had cried for a few hours after I found it, my fingers running along the note repeatedly as I tried to picture him writing it.

Our shared birthday was exactly two weeks after he had died. Mark rarely buys me a present, but when he does I knew that he always tried to hide it the last place that I would expect. I guess this time he had settled on putting my present right underneath my nose.

My brother knew me best though, so he was right. This was the book that changed everything. It was a simple love story about a boy and girl who meet in school and how they overcome all of their ups and downs and somehow come out on the other side holding hands. It was sweet, a little cheesy, but my brother thought that I would like it so I did.

I guess that's why I ended up in the library on my lunch on the second day back to school. During math I had convinced some girl with glasses that were too big for her head and bright green braces to sit next to me, ensuring that Elli didn't have an opportunity to talk to me.

Lunch though, was lonely. I almost wished that someone would find me and bother me just so that I could use my voice a little bit. Rather, I was sitting alone in the library taking rabbit bites out of a turkey sandwich that I had made the night before.

"I thought you didn't read books?"

My head snapped up and my gaze settled on Carter who was standing at the opposite side of the table that I was currently sitting at. He had a small smirk on his face and his eyes looked like they were taunting me. My gaze settled on my book that I held open with my free hand; my other hand occupied by my sandwich.

I didn't want to answer him, but I knew that I had wished for someone to talk to- obviously I hadn't specified for it not to be Carter- yet at this point I would take what I could get. Plus, the feeling of butterflies that I got in my stomach whenever I talked to Carter felt extremely appealing and irresistible. In that moment I wanted to talk to him because I wanted to feel happy.

Yet the events of the past summer replayed over and over again in my head, and I quickly built up my barrier that had started to crumble. Instead of responding I simply shrugged.

"I'm sorry about yesterday." He offered, taking a couple of steps closer towards me.

My eyes hopped from bookshelf to bookshelf that came into my view over his shoulder instead of meeting his eyes. I shrugged again, my fingers playing with the edge of the book. Folding the corner back and forth. Back and forth. Back and forth.

"Zo, look at me."

Immediately I slammed my book shut and stood up slowly. "Don't you dare call me Zo."

He looked hurt for a second before he covered the look back up with a blank face. "Zoe, I wanted to apologize."

"For what? The past two months? Or for yesterday?"

This time Carter didn't bother trying to cover up his emotions, I saw confusion and anger flash across his face before he finally settled on just looking hurt. "I did nothing-"

"Save it." I shoved my book into my bag along with my half eaten sandwich, "I don't want to hear your excuses."

I slung one strap of my backpack over my shoulder and attempted to maneuver my way past him. Carter found a way to block me in though, stepping between the book case and the table leaving no way out.

"Don't be ridiculous, Carter. Class is about to start."

I once again tried to shove my way past him, pushing my shoulder against his. Although he had a good three inches and fifty pounds on my slim frame so I was no match for him. "Carter, please. Just let me go." My voice cracked on the last sentence and that's when Carter finally gave in. He stepped to the side, not saying another word as I walked past him and out of the library.

I was in a foul mood when I finally got home that Tuesday night. My plan to change seats in English in order to avoid sitting next to Carter was ruined when Mr. Smith insisted that we sit in the same seats as the day before.

It didn't seem to matter though; it was like I wasn't sitting next to him anyway. Carter didn't say anything to me, he wasn't trying to be sweet like he was in the library nor was he snapping at me like the day before. Instead, he was just silent.

I was okay with the silent treatment, if I never talked to him again for as long as I lived I would be perfectly content. Although it was a little unnerving because the old Zoe seemed to be poking her head through the cracks in the wall that I had built saying I want to forgive you Carter! Please just talk to me.

Luckily I was able to keep my mouth shut, only speaking when spoken to and even then my answers were just simple yes and no's.

My mood only deteriorated when I arrived at my locker at the end of the day to find Elli and Henry- her new boyfriend I assumed; a conclusion that I came to after seeing them kiss yesterday- leaning against my locker.

"Excuse me." I had asked, motioning towards my locker. "I need to get my stuff."

Elli shook her head before giving Henry a knowing look. "We want to talk to you."

Where were you when I wanted to talk to you? I was half tempted to ask but instead I just said, "I have nothing to say to either of you, or for Carter for that matter."

Elli sighed, reaching out and grabbing my hand with hers. "We-I just want to know that you're okay. You're still my best friend, Zoe."

I pulled my hand away, not making eye contact. If I did, I had known that she would see that I didn't mean what I said next. But I wanted my words to have the desired impact, "You're not mine, though."

They left without saying another word and I was left alone in front of my locker. A horrible feeling had come over me in the moment, a feeling of guilt and frustration mixed together, and the feeling was still with me now.

"You're home." The sound of Mom's voice pulled me out of my thoughts, bringing me into the present.

I nodded, throwing my backpack down beside the door. This was the extent of me and my mother's conversations since Mark's death, if we did any talking at all. My dad on the other hand, was another story.

"Sweetie!" I turned to look at the top of the stairs where he was standing, looking at me with a large smile. All I saw in his eyes were pride, nothing like the sadness that filled my mother's.

I returned the smile as well as I could, running up the stairs to meet him halfway for a hug. With his arms wrapped around me I pulled back a little bit to look at his face, although he looked just as tired as my mom did, he hid it better than her, "You've been gone for so long." I finally said; my heart squeezing as I looked over my dad.

My dad let me go and wrapped his arm around my shoulder instead, steering me back down the stairs. "Work got in the way," He shrugged, his hand squeezing my shoulder as he talked, "what matters is that I'm here now." Dad cocked his head towards the front door; his eyes were all ready shining with that look that he got before a challenge. "Want to go shot some hoops?"

"Dad, I have homework."

"Come on, we can do first person to twenty- that won't take too long. Plus, you get to spend time with your favourite man." He nudged me twice with his elbow, almost daring me to come and play.

I raised my eyebrows; this was not my favourite idea of how I could spend time with my father. I preferred the moments when he sat on the couch doing the crossword from the Sunday newspaper and I sat next to him playing on my phone, my head on his shoulder. Or, I loved when we would just go for drives around the neighbourhood pointing out different things to each other; like Christmas light during the winter, or the gorgeous gardens, or the people taking their dogs on a walk. That was more like my ideal bonding time with my father.

"I don't do sports Dad."

"Come on, Zo. It'll be fun."

By now he had lead me over to the front door. Dad was already slipping on his running shoes and the sweatshirt that he called his 'game saver' because he had never lost a basketball game back in high school without it.

"Go on, sweetheart." I looked up and saw my mom standing in the adjoining family room, her hands resting on the back of the couch. "I'll make you both a snack for when you come inside."

"See," My Dad beamed with his hand resting on the door knob, "homework can wait. Let's go play."

His joyous personality was infectious, and shortly thereafter I found myself slipping on my running shoes and joining him.

For a moment, when I scored and he came over and lifted me off the ground-spinning me around and around and around- I could pretend that this was our tradition, our game. But deep in the back of my mind I could hear the little voice reminding me that this wasn't our thing, this was his and Mark's Saturday morning tradition.

I would always be the one sitting on the porch and watching them play, laughing as my Dad pretended to get angry when Mark scored but secretly he would turn around with a smile. Mark was Dad's mini-me; my dad practically sculpted him to be that way since we were born.

We all learned to grieve and move on in our own ways, and for my Dad to move on he needed to learn how to fill the holes that Mark had left behind when he died- and I suppose he was trying to fill some of those holes with me.

CHAPTER 3

"Group work is a requirement in this English course, we have been told that we must have at least one group project per class; I have plans to do at least three. The first project that I'm about to assign will be done in pairs."

Almost immediately a hand shot up, obviously about to ask the question that was on the tip of everyone's tongue. Mr. Smith sighed when he saw the hand, but nonetheless pointed towards the student. "Do we get to pick our partners?"

My stomach was in knots as I awaited his answer. My hope was that the answer would be no, my worst fear would be sitting here waiting for someone to approach me- or even worse, me having to approach someone else. Although, that would be better than being partnered with a certain someone who was eagerly waiting Mr. Smith's answer along with the rest of the class.

We were well into our second week back to school. Carter, Elli and the rest of my old group of friends had finally relented in trying to renew our friendship and I had been spending most of my lunches in the library and the rest of my time was spent wandering the hallways alone with my head down.

Mr. Smith cleared his throat and ran his finger under his collar before speaking, "Well, I have already assigned your partners." Almost instantaneously a groan came from the class, I remained silent. "Now; before anyone complains- I'm not going to change any partners unless there are drastic reasons, and by drastic I mean your partner tried to murder your dog- or something along those lines." The class let out a half-hearted laugh at his joke.

He grabbed a single sheet of paper from the top of his desk, "I'll read out your partners and then hand out the assignment so that we can go over it together, please try and remain as quiet as you can while I read out the list."

The class was silent as we waited for him to tell us our partners, eager to know who we would be put with.

"Mathew and Daniel."

"Amy and Caitlin."

"Josh and Elizabeth."

"Sarah and Paul."

"Carter and-"He paused. Please don't be me. Please don't be me. Please don't be me. "Zoe." It was me.

I could feel Carters gaze slowly shift from Mr. Smith to me and back again. I continued to stare straight ahead, hoping that this was some sort of mistake.

The class passed by slowly after that, as Mr. Smith explained that we were to create a fifty minute presentation based on certain pre-assigned themes. I held my breath when Mr. Smith told us to get together with our partners and begin to make plans for our presentations.

"I'll tell him that this isn't going to work." My head snapped around to meet Carter's scrutinizing gaze, "Unless you don't want me to?" He asked, cocking his head to the side. Carter was taunting me, he was trying to get me to say no because he knew the last thing that I wanted was to agree with him.

"Of course, we can talk to him after class." It hurt to say it but I did, slowly I turned back to look ahead again; my eyes focusing on nothing as I waited for the bell to ring.

When the bell finally rung we approached Mr. Smith while the rest of our peers were leaving the classroom and by the look on his face it seemed he knew what we were going to ask. "I think that this paring will be good for you." He told us before we even got a chance to open our mouths.

I resisted the urge to roll my eyes, already knowing how this argument would end. "Sir, unfortunately Carter and I don't get along and I don't want my mark to suffer-"

Mr. Smith held up his hand, cutting off the speech that I had pre-planned in the moments before class had ended. "Like I just said," He told us, packing his laptop into his briefcase which was sitting on his chair. "I think that this would be good for you both."

"Mr. Smith, I don't want my mark to suffer either and working with Zoe will be nearly impossible." Carter added.

Mr. Smith laughed as he slung the strap of his laptop case across his shoulder, "Nearly impossible does not mean completely impossible." He patted Carter on the shoulder and gave me a smile, "Good luck on the project you two, I'm excited to see what you come up with." Then he left, leaving Carter and I alone in the classroom.

"I can do the entire thing and you can put your name on it." I said quickly, not making eye contact with Carter.

Carter sighed, grabbing his binder off of his desk before walking back to where I was standing at the front of the classroom. "Can we just split the project 50/50 and then combine the work that we did into one presentation?"

"I don't think this is a project that works like that Carter," I glanced wistfully at the door, wishing that we could hurry with this conversation so that I could go home as quickly as possible, "Just let me do the project, okay? I won't tell him." I started backing slowly towards the door, hoping that was the end of our conversation.

Carter reached out and grabbed my arm, successfully stopping me about a foot before the classroom door. "I can't let you do that, Zoe." I knew by the look in his eyes that he wasn't going to back down, "Come to my place Friday night and we can work on it together, alright?"

I tried to ignore the tingles I felt radiating from the spot where Carter was holding me, "Carter, I don't think that's such a good idea. You know-"

He cut me off, "I'll see you Friday night." Then he walked out of the classroom, leaving me alone and, quite frankly, confused.

I met Carter Jacobs when we were both five. Actually, I was five and he was five and a half- as he reminded me more times than I could possibly count over the course of our friendship.

Carter had been friends with my brother first. In kindergarten the school thought that it would be a good idea to put Mark and I in separate classrooms, so that we could 'branch out and make new friends'. My parents agreed with them and inevitably- despite Mark and I's persistent arguments- we were split up.

Mark and Carter were in the same class and they seemed to gravitate towards each other. It wasn't long until I was hearing about Carter nearly every day at dinner and they became self-proclaimed best friends. After nearly two months of constant stories about Carter, who I think my parents were beginning to think wasn't actually a real person, he was invited for a sleepover.

I first laid my eyes on Carter when his parent's dropped him off for his and Mark's first sleepover. I was the one to open the door for him and as soon as I saw him I fell in love, and I'm pretty sure he smiled because he felt it too.

I spent my entire weekend trailing around Carter and Mark, taking notes in my messy five year old scrawl about Carter's behavior and the things that I supposedly 'loved' about him. I don't know where the notes went, I shoved it somewhere that Mark couldn't find it and I guess that I hid it so well that I wasn't able to find it myself.

Either way, over the course of that weekend, Carter had squeezed his way into my life. Even then, I knew that he would change my life- only I never knew how severely.

"I'm going out." I called out into my quiet house, my hand already resting on the door handle, "I'll be back in a couple of hours."

Excepting no response, as was the usual these days, I prepared to leave but stopped when I heard a voice call back to me. "Where are you going?" My mum asked, poking her head out from the kitchen.

I silently cursed myself for not being faster before stepping back into the house. "I was going to head over to West Side."

West Side was a small café that connected onto a library; it was located in downtown Toronto. We lived in a suburb of Toronto called Riverrun, within walking distance to the subway that took you straight to downtown Toronto. My parent's never liked me going downtown on my own and they always insisted that Mark went with me. As a result of this, I hadn't made the trip to West Side since his death.

"You know that we don't like you going on the subway on your own." Mum reminded me, wiping her hands on a cloth. "Especially since it's going to be dark out soon."

"Who do you want me to go with Mom? Mark's gone and I don't exactly have any friends that I can call to come with me." I felt my mood go from calm to angry quickly.

"Well, that's not what I was suggesting-"

I rolled my eyes, already turning back towards the door, "I'm going to go now Mum, you're more than welcome to come if you want but honestly it's not like I'm going to die."

"Don't talk to me like that, Zoe." She placed her hands on her hips and I could tell that she was slowly getting more angry, "I am your mother whether you like it or not."

"Really, Mum? Because it seems like you stopped being a mother when Mark died." My blood was boiling and I knew that if I didn't get out of there soon enough I was going to burst and the end result was not going to be pretty. "I'll see you when I get back." I slammed the door behind me and practically ran down the street in fear that my mum would follow me, but when I looked back the door had remained closed.

The subway was not my favourite place in the world. I was a self-diagnosed germaphobe and the amount of germs on the subway was not something that I liked to think about, just moments earlier I had seen someone sneeze into their hand and then wipe it along the handle bar. Needless to say I had both my hands shoved into my pockets and I remained as close to the subway car door as I possibly could so that I would be the first person off of the train.

As soon as the automated voice announced the name of my stop I practically threw myself through the subway doors, careful not to brush up against anyone as I did. The smell of stale pee hit me as I walked throw the lower level of the subway station, I scrunched up my nose in distaste and began my trek up the stairs to the main street.

Toronto was no doubt my favourite place in the world; I was reminded why when I came out at the top of the stairs from the subway station. Almost immediately the smell of pee was replaced with the smell of hot dogs and hamburgers and the loud noises of cars honking and people yelling into their cell phones.

I took it all in, letting the feel of city life overwhelm me before I began walking in the direction of West Side. I hadn't been lying when I told my mother that was where I was going; it had been my intent to go there since school had started this year. It was a yearly tradition of mine and Mark's- and then eventually Carter, Elli and the rest of our small group of friends- that began as soon as we were old enough to go on the subway without our parents.

We didn't have a specific day that we would go; instead we would go whenever we were craving it or needed the time away from our parents. Today I was going for a different reason.

West Side is one of the places that I remembered Mark constantly being happy- I wanted to remember him laughing in our favourite booth in the corner, his coffee spilling slightly whenever he would laugh to hard; or when he accidentally let it slip that he might just be in love with his girlfriend Jenny when we were ten years old- they broke up after a month. I wanted these memories to be mine. Not like at home, where I shared the memories with my parents. Or at school, where all of my fellow peers and teachers remembered him to. No, at West Side- even if it wasn't always just me and him here, these memories were still almost exclusively mine.

I stopped short when I saw the familiar green sign of the café, blaring at me from where I stood not twenty feet away. The last time I had been here had been with Mark, only a few days before he died. We had been celebrating surviving exams. Today though, I wasn't celebrating.

I walked towards the door slowly, already regretting my decision to come here. Eventually I made it inside of the café, my senses being overwhelmed by the smell of coffee and the quiet murmur of people talking. Towards my right was the entrance to the library, where I normally ventured while Mark bought our drinks, but today I made my way into the purchase line.

"Hello there, how can I help you today?"

I looked up at the menu, tempted to order my regular hot chocolate but instead decided to buy Mark's favourite; he had practically preached the coffee that was called 'Canadiano', a play on the popular 'Americano'.

"I'll just have a medium Canadiano, with extra whipped cream and cinnamon please." I reached into my wallet and began scrounging around for the change to pay, already knowing what the total would be.

"Will that be all for today?"

I placed the change on the counter before she could tell me, "Yes, thank you."

"Alright you're total is –"

"$2.35." Myself and the cashier said at the same time.

She laughed, reaching for the change. "I assume you've ordered this before?"

I was ready to correct her, telling her that this was my first time ordering but it was refreshing to be talking to someone my age who didn't necessarily know my whole back story. "Something like that." I settled on, taking the coffee from her before wishing her a good day and heading over to my regular booth.

I chose to sit facing towards the café, playing with the lid of my coffee cup as I waited for it to cool down a little bit.

It was strange as it was my first time visiting West Side on my own, but for some reason I didn't feel alone. If I closed my eyes I could almost feel Mark sitting there next to me; and unlike at school, the feeling wasn't unsettling, rather it was comforting. So I allowed myself to settle on into the booth and pretend like Mark really was there with me.

CHAPTER 4

I loved naps. They were a rare treat in my household, so when you had the opportunity to shut your eyes for twenty minutes you took it.

That was the situation that I found myself in on Friday night. I had finished some homework and my parent's were still not home so I figured that I may as well use my time wisely and take a nap. Unfortunately, there came a point where you had to be woken up- and needless to say my wake up call that night wasn't the best.

Bring, Bring

"Can someone please get that?"

Bring, Bring

"Lillian, is that your phone?"

Bring, Bring

"No Jack, isn't that yours?"

Bring, Bring

"Nope, not mine. Maybe it's Zoe's? Zoe! Check your phone, sweetie."

Bring, Bring

"Zoe, if you don't answer your phone I'm going to come up there."

Bring, Bring

"ZOE!"

Bring, Bri-

"I've got it." I shot up in bed, my hand slamming down on my phone in an attempt to make it stop and inadvertently answering the phone call instead. I ran a hand through my hair in frustration before grabbing the already answered phone, "Hello?" I croaked into the speaker while rubbing a finger along the corner of my eyes in an attempt to get the sleep out of my eyes.

"Zoe? Where are you?" The man on the other end asked, I frowned-wondering why I hadn't thought to check the caller idea.

I rolled over in my bed and took a quick glance at the time on the clock; 8:17 at night. Had I really been sleeping that long? "Who is this?"

"It's Carter." I could tell by tone of his voice that he was frustrat-ed, "You were supposed to be here over an hour ago."

"Oh God, I'm so sorry." I ran a hand across my forehead, won-dering how I could have possibly forgotten. I had been stressed about this day since the incident in the classroom earlier that week. "I must have fallen asleep. Give me ten minutes and I'll be right over."

"Don't worry; I'm waiting in my car outside. Just be quick, we need to get at least some work done tonight." Before I had a chance to beg him to reschedule, he hung up.

Slowly I pulled myself out of my bed. Using my index finger and thumb, I pulled open the curtains, and sure enough his car was parked in the street outside of my house. "Son of a-"

"Language, Zoe. We raised you better than that." When I turned around my mother was standing in the doorway, her hands on her hips. "Who was that on the phone?"

"Carter; he's waiting outside for me." I groaned when the hair brush refused to run all of the way through my hair, getting caught on multiple knots along the way. I settled on throwing it up into a bun in hopes that would hide all of the knots.

I smoothed out the wrinkles in my sweater, trying to make it look like I hadn't just been drooling all over my pillow moments earlier. "Oh, so you two are friends again?" Mum asked hesitantly, still leaning against the doorway.

"No, we got partnered together for a project and we need to work on it. I'll be back in an hour or two." I said, finally semi-okay with my appearance. "Can you leave the door unlocked?"

"Of course," She said with a small smile on her face. Mum tucked a strand of loose hair behind my hair when I came to stand in front of her, "Have fun, honey."

"Mum-It's a school project. I don't think we're really allowed to have fun."

She laughed lightly, "I know just-Just don't forget that it's okay to be happy sometimes, you deserve it."

"What was our topic again?" Carter asked. He was lying on his back on the bed, looking up at the ceiling.

I sighed, cringing like I had multiple times before, "Love." I was walking around his room, inspecting his posters and all the miscellaneous items that looked like they hadn't been touched since I had last been here.

I stopped short when I saw a picture of myself, Mark and Carter at a carnival when we were about ten. Our parents had taken us for the day one weekend. I remember being so excited to go on the Ferris Wheel with my brother but he had gotten sick after we went on a rollercoaster and my hopes for the Ferris Wheel were nearly shattered, until Carter agreed to go with me. It was my favourite part from our trip to the carnival, and I owed it all to Carter.

"That was a fun day." Carter commented while pointing at the picture I was looking at.

I gave the picture one last look before I turned around to face him, "So, do you have any ideas?"

He shrugged, his eyes leaving me to go to the ceiling again. I let my gaze dance around the room so I wouldn't be inclined to look at the strip of stomach that Carter was showing-his shirt had risen slightly when he had laid down on his bed and I could not stop staring at it. "Well, I think we should call it a night. We've done enough work for today." He sat up suddenly in his bed, his shirt falling down to cover his stomach.

"We just got started, Carter." Either way I was secretly jumping inside at the thought of getting home, if I was lucky there would still be enough time for me to watch my favourite show and then have a nice warm bubble bath afterwards.

"Yeah, but I don't think either of us really want to do this right now."

I wanted to argue with him- probably just for the sake of arguing, we had been getting along almost too well tonight-but instead I just nodded, gathering my backpack from its spot on his desk. "Well, I guess I'll see you later then?"

He reached out and grabbed my arm before I could slip through his bedroom door. I gave the hallway a longing look before I was pulled back into his bedroom. I should have known that he had something else in mind.

"Actually, I invited some people over to hang out. You should stick around."

I ripped my arm from his grasp and placed my hands on my hips before shooting him a glare that I knew would get my message across, "You invited people over when you knew we'd be working on our project? I should have known you wouldn't want to do school work on a Friday night."

"Zoe, I-"He was cut short by the sound of someone knocking on the door. Carter groaned, running a hand through his hair, "Please just stick around for a little bit."

"Carter," I pleaded, "Take me home."

"Fine," He grabbed his black jacket from where he had thrown it on his floor after he came to pick me up, "Just come down with me and I'll let them in then we can go."

"Okay." I agreed, I knew that I would still have to face our friends when I went downstairs, but at least Carter wouldn't make me actually socialize. I took a deep breath before I followed Carter down the stairs.

"It should just be Elli and Henry," Carter told me as he put on his coat.

"That doesn't make it any better." I grumbled, standing behind him as we got closer to the front door. I could see the silhouettes of more than just two people through the curtain.

Carter opened the front door before I had the chance to complain and standing in front of us had to be at least ten people. "Shit," Carter looked over his shoulder at me and then back to the people waiting outside his front door, "I didn't invite this many people I swear."

"Just get me out of here." I moaned into his shoulder suddenly wishing that I had slept through his phone call earlier that night.

"Are you going to let us in our what?" That was John; he was the self-proclaimed 'partier' of the group. If you ever wanted someone to throw a party for you he was the man to go to. Mark had called up John more times than I could count over the years, and John had been the host of a little party in honour of Mark after he died- I hadn't gone.

"Yeah, C, we can't wait out here all night." Kyle added. I had seen a flash of his flaming red hair when Carter had opened the front door, so I knew that he would be there.

I was still hoping that they couldn't see, I had practically buried myself into Carter's back and my hope was that they were oblivious enough not to notice a person behind him.

Unfortunately, I underestimated their deduction skills because I heard my name being called out only seconds later. "Zoe!" It was Ryder, the quietest one in the group- he was shy, but not when he was around his friends. I let out a sigh and slowly took a couple of steps so that I was standing beside Carter instead of behind him. "I thought that was you." Ryder beamed. He reached forward to give me a hug but I quickly took a step back before he could.

"I was just about to drive Zoe home," Carter said, saving me from having to say something to Ryder, "You guys can come in and make yourself at home, I'll be back in ten minutes."

I adverted my eyes to the ground as they all piled into the house, each person saying some sort of hello to me but I remained quiet. A part of me missed these people; I missed the Friday night get-togethers. Yet another part of me was missing- that part had been taken when Mark died- and I wasn't the same person that I used to be.

Soon it was only Carter and I standing next to the front door. I was a little hurt that Elli hadn't said a word to me when she passed, but I knew that I had no right to be upset. So with one last glance at the family room, I followed Carter out of the house and into the car.

CHAPTER 5

When someone close to you dies, it feels like you're heart is ripped out of your chest and stomped on repeatedly. There isn't a part of you that doesn't hurt and you cry so much that you think you'll never be able to cry again.

This isn't the type of pain that goes away either, its there- tucked away, waiting for the day that something triggers it. It's a raw pain that can hit you when you least expect it, you can be doing something as simple as grocery shopping when you see something that reminds you of them and suddenly you can't breathe because it hurts so bad.

My eyes had finally fluttered shut the night that Carter had dropped me off at home when it smelt it. I knew that smell; I had smelt it more times than I could count. It was Mark's cologne.

It wasn't long before the aching feeling hit me; it started in the back of my throat and slowly spread up to behind my eyes. It didn't take much until the aching feeling hurt so much that I began dry heaving and moments later my mother was in the room, her arms wrapped around my shoulders as I tried my hardest to catch my breath.

"You're okay," She whispered, her face buried into my shoulder as her one hand stroked my hair, "Shh, Zoe. You're alright."

Eventually I was able to breathe normally and the aching feeling slowly subsided.

My eyes drifted to look at my mother, who had stopped with the comforting words but was still holding me. I felt so safe in her arms that for that night I just let her hold me.

She was one of the only people who truly understood my pain, and she knew that at that moment all that I needed was to feel her arms around me. It didn't take long before my eyes fell shut and I was asleep.

The coffee shop became somewhat of a safe haven for me over the following weeks. When I was stressed, I went to West Side. When I was upset, I went to West Side. When I was confused, I went to West Side.

When I had woken up this morning I hadn't felt anything. Instead, I just felt empty. Incredibly, incredibly empty.

So, I decided to go to West Side.

I had become a regular here, so I wasn't surprised when I walked in the waitress gave me a smile and a kind hello instead of asking what I would like to order. It had become routine, I went and sat in the corner booth and she brought the drink over to me.

I was settling into the booth when I felt a presence at the end of the table; I looked up and sucked in a sharp breath. Standing at the end of my table was Thea, Mark's-Actually; I didn't know what to call her. They had been dating for nearly two years when Mark had died. She was absolutely devastated. Yet calling her his girlfriend seemed morbid.

"Hi." She gave me a soft smile, if Thea was one thing, it was kind. She was so incredibly kind that it almost hurt me when I started turning her away. One day, a week or so after Mark passed; I just stopped answering her calls. I hadn't seen her since the funeral.

"I didn't expect to see you here." Thea said, tucking a strand of her straight blond hair behind her ear. "I-Um, I've been coming here since-Um, you know." She cast her eyes towards the counter in obvious discomfort, "I was a little shocked to see someone sitting in this booth because-"Thea stopped talking suddenly and her eyes slowly came back to mine, "Can I sit down?"

I simply nodded. I didn't know what to say to her, I never really knew what to say to her. She loved Mark in a way that I could never understand because I had never experienced that kind of love, and I had no idea how it felt to have that love taken away from you.

"I work here now." Thea offered, trying to start the conversation as she placed her palms flat on the table. "I thought that it was one way for me to-you know, move on?" There was a pause then, "How are you?" She said it so seriously that I knew I wasn't going to get away with an answer like 'good' or 'I'm doing well, and you?' because she knew. She had lost the same person that I had.

"I'm not so-"

I was about to tell her everything, I really was. I was going to tell her how I struggled to wake up in the mornings and sometimes in the middle of the night I would have these horrible panic attacks because I had a dream that Mark had been taken away from me once more. I was going to tell her that I think I was falling back and love with Carter and how absolutely terrified I was because I never wanted to experience the pain of losing someone ever again. Most of all, I was going to reveal just how guilty I felt for feeling that way about Carter.

I was going to tell her all of that and more; but I was interrupted by the waitress who beamed down at us with two cups of coffee in her hands.

"Two Canadiano's with extra whipped cream and cinnamon." She placed a cup in front of Thea and I respectively before leaning back on her heels, "Anything else I can get you two?"

We both politely declined and she let us be.

Thea turned to look back at me and I couldn't help but notice what a strong contrast her blonde hair was against the bright blue colour of the booth. "You were going to say-"

I was going to tell you exactly how I felt, Thea. I was going to open up to you more than I had opened up to anyone over the past four months. I was going to tell you how I was really feeling because deep down inside I actually wanted to tell someone that I might have been broken but I was ready to start healing. But instead I said, "I'm doing okay."

Thea left when she finished her cup of coffee. She had tried to get me to tell her more in depth about how I was feeling but I totally closed off, letting my emotionless mask slip on as she hammered me with questions.

Eventually she got tired, and decided that it was time to go.

"I just finished my shift," She had said, placing her hands over mine which we currently folded on the table, "I work here most days of the week and anytime you want to talk-anytime-I'm here. I-"She paused and let out a shaky breath before she whispered, "I understand, Zoe. I can just listen if you'd like."

I pulled my hands away and Thea's hands fell to the table. "I'm alright. Really, Thea, I am."

"Alright." She slipped on her coat and slid out of the booth, "My number's the same, anytime you need me you call-okay Zoe?"

I was ready to protest but I knew agreeing would send her away quicker so instead I settled on, "I know where you are, Thea."

Now I was alone; sitting in the booth with my hands wrapped around my third cup of coffee. It was frustrating how much I craved companionship, because- I'd come to realize- not only was I alone, I was also lonely.

There's an incredibly difference between being alone and being lonely. Right now, technically speaking, I wasn't alone. A few teenagers were in line waiting to order coffee and at least three waitresses were busy behind the counter of coffee shop. So, in the space of the coffee shop I was not alone-but I was alone in my booth.

Lonely, on the other hand, was incredibly different. Lonely meant that no matter how many people were around you during the day, you still felt like you were alone. Loneliness was this aching feeling that followed me around during the day because I craved the feeling of company even if I had it. I craved the friendship that I once had with Elli and Carter and the constant feeling of trust that came along with it.

I was still sitting there, my coffee slowly turning cold, when Carter and a few others came pouring into the coffee shop. Their cheeks were tinged red and I knew that the chill I had felt this morning had only gotten worse. Fall was well on its way.

Just my luck. I cringed when Carter's eyes began roaming around the shop, his eyes getting closer and closer to the booth; and his eyes were about to fall right on me when-

"Carter!" It was a girl named Olivia; she was pretty- a small nose, hazel eyes and medium length brown hair. She and I had never been friends, it was a mutual understanding that we just didn't click. I had always thought that Olivia and Carter didn't get along either but her hand was on his chest as she stared up to him with this expression filled with what looked like love.

Carter, on the other hand, was looking at her with that indifferent look of his.

"Aren't you going to order?" She giggled in that high pitch voice of hers, her Bambi eyes widening as she waited eagerly for his response. She looked like a dog waiting to be acknowledged by their owner.

He placed his hand slowly on top of hers and pushed it away, "I'll order when I'm ready." He stepped up to the counter, manoeuvring his way around Olivia as he did. "One Canadiano with extra whipped cream and cinnamon, please."

"Oh, wow." The girl at the counter exclaimed, "That's like, the sixth time today someone ordered that."

Almost instantaneously he looked around to the booth in the corner, and just as quickly I ducked down. My back slid along the edge of the seat as I hid myself underneath the table, my head cramped at an uncomfortable angle while I prayed that Carter left as soon as he received his order- and that my hair wasn't stuck in a piece of gum.

"Zoe, I can see you." It was him, of course. Carter would never be as oblivious to miss my little disappearing act, mind you- the waitress probably said to him that I was just sitting at this very booth.

When I dared to open my eyes I saw his face right in front of mine, I jumped- my head hitting the table and I immediately grasped the spot where my head had connected with the hard surface. Slowly, I pulled myself out from under the table, sliding across the dirty tiled floor. A little reluctantly I pulled myself up so that I was face to face with Carter.

I knew that my face was a deep shade of red when Carter's lips twitched at the corners, he always thought that it was cute when I blushed- I, on the other hand, only became more embarrassed and would turn an even darker shade of red- if that was even possible.

"Why were you under the table?" He rocked back on his heels when he said it, his eyes teasing me. Carter could be such an egoistic jerk sometimes, I thought repeatedly, thinking of different ways that I could kill.

I shrugged, not meeting his eyes, while I kicked at invisible dirt. "I-Um, I dropped my fork."

"Fork?" I knew that he was trying his hardest not to laugh, "But why did you need a fork? You weren't eating any food."

I wanted to return back under the table when he said that, why did I say I dropped my fork? But instead I met his gaze head on and tried to appear much more confident that I really was, "Carter, I've had a long day-I mean, I just had to deal with Thea-"

"Thea was here?" The smile slipped off of his face, "How is she?"

I shook my head, not believing the turn for the worse that my day had taken. Faintly, in the background, I could hear Olivia jabbering away about some teacher that had given her a seventy percent when she clearly deserved a perfect grade.

It was times like these that I hated my brother for dying. I knew that it wasn't his fault, he didn't choose this. Yet I wish that I was able to go back to when I was so careless; when the only worries I had were whether my hair looked good or the cute boy in my grade really did have a crush on me. Instead, I was worried about having to talk to my dead brother's girlfriend.

"Fine." I said finally, when I realized that Carter was still waiting for an answer. Except Thea wasn't fine, I wasn't fine and I was almost positive that Carter wasn't fine. His eyes didn't shine as

brightly as they had when I had slowly fallen in love with him-
first when we were five years old, then again at ten and one final
time at fifteen.

Now, at seventeen- I realized that I had grown to hate those
eyes, not love them- as I had almost told Thea earlier. I hated
that he felt broken. I hated that a piece of him was missing too.
I absolutely hated that Carter had survived, that he was here to
order Mark's favourite coffee, here to talk about Thea.

Most of all; I hated that Carter was the reason that my brother
was dead.

CHAPTER 6

I was over at Elli's- talking about my turbulent love life, or something along those line- when I first learned that my brother was dead. My mom didn't even try to sugar coat it on the phone, "He's dead." was all that she said before I had dropped the phone on to the floor.

I remember thinking that he couldn't possibly dead- not my brother. Not Mark, with eyes the same colour as mine. Not my brother who had punched the first boy that had broken my heart. Not my brother who pretended to be a bad boy, when in reality he cried during Titanic. Not my brother, who was on his way to Elli's house with Carter at that very moment. Not. My. Brother.

It was, though. I had Elli drive me to the hospital, where I found my parents standing in the waiting room. My mother was pulling away from my father, who was trying to wrap her in a hug. They both looked so broken.

Hesitantly I walked to them, my feet dragging against the slick tile floor- I didn't want them to say it again. I wanted to them to say that he wasn't dead; he was actually upstairs in one of those too small hospital rooms, watching some silly cartoon on the television with his goofy smile on his face.

He wasn't though, of course he wasn't.

"What happened?" I asked, my voice barely a whisper. I didn't want to know the answer, but we were all sitting so quietly in the waiting room that I needed to say something.

"He was drunk." My Dad answered, his voice lacking his normal enthusiasm, "Drunk driving. Carter, he- The car just hit them on the passenger side and they spun and hit a telephone pole- God, he ran a red because he was fucking drunk."

That was all that I had, I didn't want to hear any more and my parents never offered to fill in the holes of the story of what happened that night. All that I knew was that my brother was dead because Carter got behind the wheel drunk.

I knew that it probably wasn't totally Carter's fault- Mark had a way of getting people to drink with him when he wanted them too. But Carter should have never gotten behind the wheel.

As intoxicating as Carter was, that wasn't something that I was able to forgive so easily.

"I want a job."

The girl behind the counter looked up; she had been engrossed in a Nicholas Sparks book and hadn't seen me come in. Her hesitation to respond didn't put me off though, I had become determined to get this job if it was the last thing that I did.

"Zoe?" Thea came out of the back room of West Side, wiping her hands on her apron as she looked at me with a questioning gaze, "you want a job?"

I nodded, hoping that my determination showed. When I had seen how this job had helped Thea move on, I decided that this was exactly what I needed.

Thea sighed, running a hand through her hair before nodding towards the booth in the corner. "I'll meet you over there in a second."

I listened to her command, slowly making my way over the booth. I could hear Thea having a hushed conversation with her co-worker, telling her that she was about to take her break. Not a minute later, two cups of hot chocolate appeared in front of me before Thea slid into the booth across from me.

"So, you want a job?"

I frowned, not too pleased with her tone of voice. "Why do you sound so reluctant?"

The soft background noise of coffee cups being filled with liquid became soothing as I waited for Thea to answer. I knew that she wouldn't want me to work, mostly because my brother was always the first one to protest me getting a job- and Thea would always back him up.

I took a sip of the hot chocolate as I waited for her to answer me.

"You can't handle this." She said finally.

"Yes I can." I nearly slammed the mug back on to the table but controlled myself before I did. I wouldn't let my anger get the best of me, not when I was trying to get a job, "I've changed, Thea." I told her in a softer voice.

She ran her hand through her hair again; it had been one of her nervous habits for as long as I had known her. I was befuddled as to why she would possibly be nervous now, though. "I know you've changed, Zoe. But I also know that this is not what you need to move on."

"I'm not trying to move on." Lie.

"Yes, you are." She fingered the handle of her mug, running her fingers up and down it multiple times before her eyes raised to meet mine. "You don't need to move on; you just need to learn how to live without him."

"I've learned how to live without Mark, look at me right now-He's gone, and I'm still living."

She shook her head, "That's not what I'm trying to say. Sure, you're alive but are you really living?"

"I-I don't understand-"

Thea gave me a sad smile, cocking her head to the side as she took in my appearance. I knew that I probably looked desperate; I was this close to getting down on my knees and beginning her to let me have this job. I needed it. I needed to know what it was like to wake up every morning and not think about Mark. By the looks of Thea, this job had helped her to forgive and forget.

"You will," Thea said, placing her hands over top of mine- Thea always tried to reassure you through touch, almost like she was getting a read on you, "And when you do, maybe we can talk about the job."

"Why can't we talk about it now?" I had to restrain myself from whining, knowing that if I did I would never get a job here. Instead, I tried to sound uninterested in her answer when in fact I knew that I was practically waiting for it like a dog waiting for its owner to give him a treat.

"Listen, my break is over and I need to get back to work- Just think about what I said alright?" With one last reassuring pat on my shoulder, Thea was gone- slipping behind the counter and into the back room.

I was disappointed to say the least. I had come into West Side so sure of myself today, positive that I would leave her as an employed woman. Instead, I was sat in the corner with a cup of hot chocolate looking like I was just shot down by the love of my life.

My eyes slowly fell on the entrance to the West Side Bookstore, which was own and run by the same people who owned the café.

Mark, when he wasn't fooling around in the booth in the back corner, could almost always be found in the book store- pouring over whatever book he was currently reading in one of the bean bag chairs on the second floor.

I found myself placing some change on the table for the hot chocolate and wandering into the book store, the tile floor under me making way to a soft beige carpet as I crossed the threshold into the store.

The store had hardly changed, other than a few new shelving units displaying new and upcoming young adult books; it looked exactly like it had before. And, luckily for myself, I knew the place like the back of my hand. Sure, I had never spent more than ten minutes inside before, but I had been in here countless times looking for Mark after I had finished shopping with Elli- which seemed to be a weekly occurrence.

Mark, like at the café, practically had a bean bag chair reserved for him on the second floor of the book store; which is where I decided to venture to. I had barely made it up the winding stair case before my path was intersected by an employee.

"Hello! How can I help you today?" I looked up and came face to face with Elli. It took me a second to realize that it was her, she had her short hair pinned back and she was wearing a pencil skirt; which is probably what surprised me the most, since Elli rarely wore anything except for jeans. The polite- and, I could tell, forced- smile slipped off of her face as she realized it was me. "Oh, Zoe. What can I do for you?"

"Um, nothing, I guess. I was just asking for a job next door and then-"I paused, my eyes flickering to the help wanted sign that I hadn't registered earlier, located conveniently on the wall next to the bathrooms. "Actually, are you guys hiring?"

I ended up leaving the book store with a book along with a promise of a call back. Elli, like Thea, had seemed reluctant to give me an application- but after I threatened to ask her manager, she caved. As I was filling out the intricate form Elli had given me a book, called Two Cups of Coffee, promising that I would enjoy it.

Hesitantly I took the book from her, praying that this wasn't her way of trying to restore our friendship. If she was willing to stand by Carter after what happened, I wouldn't be willing to stand by her. But still, the book seemed interesting and she had given it to me for free.

Now, I was cuddled up in my bed. My head was slowly sinking into my soft pillow as I waited for sleep to take over me. Instead, my mind was filled with thoughts of the book that was sitting in my bag right next to my bed.

I tried to think about other things, wondering what my cousins in California were doing right now, or when my favourite show would start airing new episodes once again. Yet for some reason my thoughts kept drifting back to that silly book.

I don't know why, maybe I was so desperate to find my therapy. Thea had her work, and I knew by the look on her face that slowly but surely she was getting over Mark. She was learning to be happy again. I wanted that, so badly that I was willing to go to great lengths to find it. I was ready- like Thea had reminded me- to not only be alive but to be happy as well.

I suppose part of me hoped that I would find it in that book.

Reluctantly, I reached over and pulled on the cord to turn on my bedside lamp, which casted a soft glow over my room. I leaned over the edge of my bed and pulled the book out of my bag, hesitantly flipping to first page. I had never been this nervous to read a book before. With one final deep breath, I began to read;

The day that Lily Knight met the love of her life, she had received news that she thought would most likely end her life, or what was left of it anyways.

Her parents had always thought that something was wrong. Lily spent the majority of her days lying in her bed doing a lot of nothing. And when she did come out, it was rare to see a smile on her face. It's a shame because Lily does have quite possibly one of the most gorgeous smiles that most people have ever seen.

When Lily's parents finally dragged her off to the doctors, she didn't complain, Lily had always wondered if there was something wrong with her. This was the best way to find out she figured.

It turned out to be depression. Her parents weren't surprised, but Lily was. She had thought that maybe she had a touch of anxiety but never in a million years did she imagine that she would have depression.

They dropped her off at the local coffee shop, telling Lily that they had to drop in to the pharmacy to pick up her prescription and that they would be right back. She didn't complain even though she wanted to. Instead, she walked up to the counter and asked for a cup of coffee.

"Make that two." A voice said from behind her. He slipped a five dollar bill onto the counter before Lily had a chance to protest, "Two cups of coffee." He repeated.

Depression.

The word was spinning around in my head, bouncing off of the walls, until it was the only word that I was thinking.

Depression.

Did Elli only give me the book because she thought that I had depression? She had even said something about Carter thinking that I would like it, had they laughed at the thought of giving this book to me behind my back?

I threw the book at the opposite wall, watching as it landed with a thud on my floor. The book wouldn't be the answer to my problems, it wasn't my magic solution. In fact, it was the furthest thing from it. The only thing that it had successfully done was make me want to retreat further into my shell.

In that moment I realized that neither Thea or Elli nor Carter for that matter, would be able to help me return to the way that I once was. They didn't care.

Learning to move on was something that I would have to do all on my own.

CHAPTER 7

My life had become incredibly repetitive. Sleep. School. Repeat. It was dull, and boring- but it was oddly comforting. Today had been another one of those repetitive days, my day passed fairly quickly with little interaction at school with anyone besides my teachers. There was a break in the pattern though, when I pulled up to my house after school. As soon as my car door opened, I was greeted by the sound of yelling.

"-she's the way she is, Lillian. You walk around all depressed and you reflect your mood on to her." I stood frozen, my hand resting on my car door as I waited to hear how my mother would respond.

"Reflect my mood on to her? Come on, Jack. I'm not allowed to grieve? My son is dead."

"He was my son too for God's sake. Why can't you remember that?"

"Are you sure that he was your son? Because you haven't acted like it. You've been gone for weeks at a time, Jesus Jack; you left on a business trip the day after Mark's funeral."

"Come on, I'm grieving too-"

"And how do you think your absence affects Zoe?"

I didn't want to hear anymore, I felt sick to my stomach just listening to the small part of their fight.

My parents had always been the picture perfect couple, married two years after they first got together in high school, pregnant with me and my brother three years after that. They were always happy, laughing, sneaking kisses- it was disgusting as a child but I knew that it was the type of love that only existed in fairytales.

This was the first time that I had ever heard them fight, and I knew that I didn't want to listen to it any further if I had to. So with one last glance at the house, I got into my car and drove off.

I didn't know where I was going. I had driven around my neighbourhood for half an hour, careful not to drive down my street, before I found myself pulling into an all too familiar driveway.

Carter's house seemed incredibly imposing from my little beat up car. I didn't know why I had come; Carter had asked if we could meet up later that night to work on our project but right now it was three thirty- not six o'clock like we had agreed upon.

I was ready to put my car in reverse and continue driving laps around the neighbourhood when the front door to the Jacobs house flew open and Carter came running down the front steps, practically sprinting towards my car. I pursed my lips when he tapped on the window, motioning for me to roll it down.

"What's the matter?" He asked, poking his head into the car. Carter's eyes seemed to be inspecting my face, dancing from my nose to my lips and back to my eyes, when he seemed satisfied that I was physically okay, he leaned back.

I focused on his fingers which were holding onto my window, like he was afraid that I would roll it up and shut him out. "Nothing's the matter."

He rolled his eyes, "Come on Zoe, I know you." It was true, he did know me. Whenever I used to be upset I used to always come running to Carter- my knight in shining armor- and I suppose that I had subconsciously come to him today.

"I'm okay."

"Then why are you here?"

I didn't answer him; instead I wrapped my fingers around the wheel. Clenching and relaxing them as I kept my eyes focused on the grey garage before me.

Carter sighed, taking his hands off of my window. "Listen, I'm about to go over to my Grandpa's- do you mind giving me a ride?"

I took my eyes off of the garage and instead turned to look at him. I knew that this was his way of trying to comfort me, something that Carter had never truly been good at, and at that moment I needed to do something to take my mind off of my parents and their fight. So I reached over and unlocked the passenger door, then motioned for him to get in.

Carter's grandfather lived on the outskirts of town, in a farm house that could easily be labeled a mansion. It had to be the largest house that I had ever seen, more bedrooms than you could ever need and nearly double the amount of bathrooms. Yet his grandfather lived there all alone.

We were halfway there when I thought of the book that Elli had given to me, Two Cups of Coffee, she had said that Carter had been the one to recommend it. I asked him why he had recommended the book for me, at this point I really didn't care why but I would do anything- or talk about anything rather- to take my mind off of what I heard from my parents.

"What book?"

He sounded genuinely confused, so I softened my voice when I said, "Two Cups of Coffee- it talks about depression a-and Elli said you recommended it for me."

Carter rolled his lip between his teeth, "Doesn't ring a bell. I'll ask Elli about it next time I talk to her."

"Okay." I murmured, dropping the subject.

The rest of the ride to his grandfather's house was silent as we both got lost in our thoughts. I couldn't stop myself from replaying the words that my parent's had said- my heart clenching when I relived the anger in their voices. It sounded like the final fight, the climax, the end. I didn't want to believe that my perfect parents could talk to each other with such hate.

When I pulled on to the gravel driveway, Carter finally broke the silence, "You're welcome to come in, Zoe."

"I-"I was ready to refuse, but then I realized that I had nowhere else to go unless I wanted to return home. "If you don't mind."

"Of course not." Carter smiled, "You know my Grandpa loves you."

We had barely made it on to the front porch when the door came flying open. Carter's grandfather looked exactly like him- same blue eyes and same stunning smile- the only difference was that his grandfather had grey hair and a few more wrinkles than Carter.

His grandfather, Gary, barely looked at Carter before his eyes settled on me. "Zoe!" He beamed, pushing back the front door a little wider, "Come on in, I haven't seen you in so long."

The house had barely changed; it still encompassed that cozy and homey feel that his wife had brought to it with her decorating skills. Since she passed away five years ago, he hadn't bought any new furniture or even moved so much as a pillow from where she had put it.

"Hi to you too, Grandpa." Carter grumbled as he followed me into the house, although he still had a small smile on his face.

"Have you two finally gotten back together?" Gary asked as Carter and I took a seat on the couches in the family room.

I chocked, not expecting that question to come out of his mouth. Gary, well not exactly quiet and shy, had always been a little conservative. Although judging by the way he raised his eyebrows at Carter, waiting for him to answer, I supposed he had changed in the six months since I had last seen him.

"Just friends, Grandpa." Carter told him, the smile on his face growing when he noticed my blush.

Gary sighed, before he clasped his hand on Carter's shoulder, "You'll have to snap that one up before it's too late."

The blush on my face had been retracting but it immediately made a comeback after that comment. My relationship with Carter had always been a touchy topic, and hearing it talked about so openly with Carter across from me was not exactly easy.

"Anyways, you wanted me to help clean out your attic?" Carter easily changed the topic when he noticed my discomfort.

Gary nodded, cocking his head towards the stairway that led upstairs. "Go on then, you know where it is."

Carter made a move towards the stairs but hesitated a few feet away, he glanced behind him and met my gaze. "Are you coming Zoe?"

As tempting as it was to sit in the family room with Gary, I couldn't stomach the thought of talking about our relationships-especially when my mind kept drifting back to my parent's marriage.

I followed him after politely declining Gary's offer of a beverage, climbing the rickety stairs to the second floor. As gorgeous and large as the house was, it was also very old. In his old age Gary had a very hard time doing the repairs by himself, insisting that Carter be the one to help him out. He wouldn't even allow Carter's father to give him a hand.

Carter reached up to pull down the stairs to the attic, which were tucked away in the ceiling of the second floor at the end of the long hallway. The stairs fell down with a bang, clambering down on to the floor. Carter immediately began dusting away the spider webs that lined the wooden stairs.

"You don't have to come up, you can stay down here if you'd like." Carter said softly, still brushing away the spider webs. It was obvious that these stairs had not been used in a while.

"I'd like to, I absolutely love antique stuff."

"I know," Carter responded, his lips turning up at the corners, "is history still your favourite subject?"

"Yeah-"I paused realizing that I had never directly told Carter that before, "How did you know?"

"I could write a book on you, Zoe Finley." He didn't give me a chance to respond, instead motioning for me to begin climbing the stairs. "I'll go up behind you, catch you if you fall."

I hesitated, eyeing the stairs wearily. "Are you sure these are safe?"

Carter shrugged, "I guess we'll see."

With a deep breath, and little reassurance from Carter, I placed my hands on the stairs and slowly began climbing. I could feel Carter behind me, his hands resting on the ladder beside my waist. I felt his finger brush against a small piece of my exposed skin on my hip as I took as I moved up, and that was all the incentive that I needed the move faster.

I let out a small breath I hadn't realized I had been holding when we reached the top, grateful to be able to put a few feet of distance between Carter and myself. "So, what exactly does Gary want us to do?"

"He wants some of these old boxes that have his pictures in them taken down so that he can sort through them and start throwing some stuff out."

My eyes danced around the attic, noticing that there had to be at least a hundred boxes in the fifteen foot by fifteen foot room. It was daunting, but I knew that Carter and I could do it.

Carter shoved his hands into his pockets and nodded towards the boxes at the right wall, "Want to split up; I'll do half, you do half and we'll meet in the middle?"

"Sure." I smiled, walking over to my side and slowly I began taking down the boxes one by one- looking inside for pictures, pushing aside the ones that didn't have any and placing the ones that did in a pile in the middle of the room.

While we didn't talk to one other over the course of the next few hours, it was an incredibly comforting silence. Even more so, I didn't think about my parents and their argument once. Subconsciously I knew that I would have to face it eventually, but it was nice to just spend the time in silence with Carter- thinking only about the work in front of me.

Moreover, I knew that afternoon that I had taken a few steps forward towards closure.

CHAPTER 8

I had come to the bleak understanding that there was, in fact, a downside to having no friends.

This realization had dawned on me when I walked into math class on Monday morning- I was early, as always, so there was only my math teacher in the class room when I arrived- and saw Mrs. Abrams separating the desks; which was something we only did when we had tests. And as far as I knew, today was not a test day.

"Oh, hello Zoe!" Mrs. Abrams beamed through the curtain of her hair, as she bent over and picked up a desk. "Are you ready for the test?"

I frowned, feeling a heavy weight come over me as I tried to recall Mrs. Abrams ever saying anything about a test. When I came up blank I simply shook my head in response to her question, holding my books closer to my chest.

"Did you study?" She questioned, separating the desks further. It was a silly countermeasure that teachers put in place to ensure that we didn't cheat, when in reality you could still easily see the test papers of our peers.

"I-I guess I forgot about the test." I stuttered before I put my books on my desk, and scrambled to grab my day planner- flipping through the dates until I reached today's date- written underneath was Math Test! I frowned, not being able to recall writing that.

She pursed her lips and ran her hand across her forehead, part of me hoped that she would be kind enough as to let me write the test tomorrow- so that I would actually have time to do at least a couple of hours of studying- but Mrs. Abrams had a firm policy on writing the test on the day it took place, and she probably wouldn't relent from it even for her star pupil. "Well, your mark shouldn't suffer to much- just try your hardest, Zoe."

I sighed, letting the flicker of hope I had go and reluctantly pulled out my chair, falling onto it. I used the few minutes of time that I had before the bell rang to flick through my notes, briefly skimming over the highlighted words in hopes of retaining some knowledge.

Lately, my head had been filled with thoughts of my parents and, as a result, I had been paying less and less attention in class- meaning that I didn't remember any of the content that I was currently trying so hard to retain.

Last week, after Carter and I had finished removing the pictures from his grandfather's attic, Carter had driven me home and I was left with the starch reality that I was going to have to face my parents. I had been reluctant to walk up the driveway, dragging my feet to postpone my entrance into the house. Only, when I opened the door I was met with darkness.

"Mum? Dad?" I called out into the dark house, expecting an answer any second.

Except it never came.

I had searched the entire house for my parents before I had come to the conclusion that they weren't there. I didn't know whether that should be a comforting thought or unsettle me further, but I still found myself crawling into bed that night- not bothering to wait up for them.

When I woke up the following morning two messages blared at me on the home screen of my cell phone;

1 Missed Call

1 Unread Messages

I frowned, unlocking my phone and reading the text message first.

From: Mum

Hi darling! Just tried to call, why aren't you answering? Isn't it time for school? Anyways, your Dad and I have decided to go away for a little while- we'll be back on Monday.

I've left some money in the cookie jar on the kitchen counter; it's only for food so don't get any ideas about parties or anything like that.

We'll call later. Love you,

Mum xoxo.

I had been confused to say the least. Not twenty four hours earlier I had heard my parents engaged in a screaming match and now they were going away together on a trip?

I had been on edge up until now, Monday- the day that they were arriving home. I had been in constant contact with my Mum over the course of their trip, yet I was still feeling unsettled about their fight.

I suppose that's why I didn't remember that we had a test today, and why I had been zoning out in all of my classes.

"Okay class, put your textbooks and binder in your desk and bring you cell phones up here. It's time to start writing your test." Mrs. Abrams informed us and she began handing out the test papers.

The thought of leaving and getting marked absent entered my head as Mrs. Abrams got closer and closer to my desk with the stack of test papers, but before I could make a move to leave she placed the test on my desk.

I reluctantly looked at the first question; Graph the reciprocal function on the graph provided below. I suppressed a groan, already confused. At this point I could only hope not to fail.

The only time that I allowed myself to smile that day was when I was standing in line waiting for lunch and my eyes fell on the abundance of food only a few feet away from me. If there was one thing that I could always count on to make me smile, it was food- as cliché as it sounded.

"I'll just have some fries please." I ordered when I was at the front of the line, the worker nodded and quickly filled some fries into a cardboard cup and handed it to me over top of the counter. Systemically I joined the queue to pay for my lunch. I fiddled with the edge of the cup, already nervous at the thought of having to choose a spot to sit.

After paying for my lunch I entered the cafeteria, scanning for an empty table. The cafeteria was dramatically lacking the seating for the amount of students who came here- so often times you were forced to share a table with people you were potentially uncomfortable with- which, when you were as antisocial as me, happened often.

I finally settled on an empty table, save for a girl who was surrounded by her binders and textbooks. I started walking in her direction, already hoping that this may be the first quiet lunch I've had since the semester started.

I coughed to get her attention when I finally came to stand at the edge of her table, my hands hovering uncertainly above a chair.

"Excuse me?" I said, my voice quiet, when she didn't respond to my cough. "Excuse me?" I repeated, a little louder.

When she didn't respond to either attempt at my getting her attention; I assumed that she either was hoping that I would go away or she genuinely couldn't hear me. I gently tapped her on her shoulder and prayed that she wasn't secretly a street fighter, although judging by her short stature and petite frame I found that possibility highly unlikely.

"Oh!" Her head flew up and her blue eyes met mine, "I'm sorry, I didn't see you there."

"I tried to get your attention a couple of times," I mumbled, tucking a piece of hair behind my hair as I avoided making eye contact. I began to think that sitting in the hallway by my locker would be more comfortable than being in this situation right now.

"I'm sorry, could you please speak up? I'm deaf in my right ear."

Immediately I stopped fiddling with my hair and I quickly made eye contact, "Really?"

She nodded, "Mmhmm, I was born like this. Anyways, you were saying?"

"I was just wondering if I could sit here." I said a little louder, hoping that she could understand me this time.

"Of course you can, only if you don't mind sitting on my left side, that way I can hear you better." Quickly she pushed aside some of her binders, making room for me so that I would be able to sit right next to her.

"I'm sorry; I don't think I caught your name."

"Zoe."

"I'm Maria." She beamed, holding her hand out for me to shake. I could tell that Maria was the enthusiastic type, one who would always find the positivity in any given situation- essentially the complete opposite to me. "Would you like to sit with me tomorrow, normally I'm left sitting on my own."

"Sure." I gave her a small smile, careful not to let it spread to big so that I wouldn't creep her out- although inside I was secretly jumping up and down for joy, here was a girl who didn't know anything about Mark; which meant that she didn't look at me with those sad eyes that I had been receiving for the past few months. It was exciting to make a new friend that had no prior preconceptions about me.

We sat in silence for the next sixty minutes, her reading through the notes in her binder- my playing Trivia Crack on my phone. At the end of lunch we exchanged a smile and a quick goodbye then proceeded to go our separate ways, yet I could tell that we formed a small friendship that day; since she understood me and I her.

So when I walked into English class later that day, I had a smile on my face- and there wasn't even food involved.

"Okay class, some people have been coming to me asking for clarification on the project." Mr. Smith told the class, his eyes sweeping over us. "So, I've decided to give it to you. I've made some revisions to the project to make it easier for you all- and I've also extended the due date." At that comment he received a loud cheer, I assumed for the most part people hadn't started the project yet.

He began to draw a mind map on the board with the word 'theme' in the middle and branches linking off of it. "You've all received a theme-"A girl in the front row raised her hand and wiggled her fingers as she attempted to get Mr. Smith's attention, "Save your questions for after class, Julia." Mr. Smith commented without turning around.

"Anyways, as I was saying you've all received a theme, from each theme you should all be able to find sub-themes. These sub-themes should have something to do with the novels that we have read in class thus far."

Beside me, Carter was tapping his pencil up and down against the desk- a steady tapping soundresounding through the classroom. I was this close to grabbing it from him and breaking it in half, clenching and unclenching my fests as I watched him smugly tap it against the wood.

"You must find a way to relate this theme to a real life situation, whether it is through pictures, a video, a PowerPoint- you decide. Now, the rest I'll leave up to you." Mr. Smith turned back to us and clapped his hands together, "Okay, pull out your novels- what page were we on?"

The tapping from beside me continued as we read through a few pages of the book as a class. I could barely focus on the words in front of me as my eyes kept drifting back to Carter's stupid pencil that repeatedly hit the desk.

"The sun reflected of the crystal blue waters, the colour reminded him of the colour of her eyes-"A girl in the class droned on, reading through the text. I stopped listening to the readings when Carter's tapping seemed to get louder and louder, my eyes narrowed in on the pencil. And then- it stopped.

I looked up and was startled to find Carter already looking at me. "Should we meet up tonight?" He whispered, careful not to catch Mr. Smith's attention.

I frowned, confused at what he was talking about. "For what?" I whispered back.

"Our project."

I pursed my lips, ready to agree but then I remembered that my parents were coming home tonight. "I can't do tonight, how about tomorrow?"

He nodded, "Works for me."

The rest of the class went on with minimal tapping from Carter and minimal listening on my part- when it came to my time to read I had to awkwardly ask Carter which page we were on, which earned me a disapproving glare from Mr. Smith.

Nonetheless, the bell soon rung and I found myself dashing out to my car in anticipation of seeing my parents. I was filled with dread at the thought but I just needed the reassurance that they were okay- that my family was okay.

My hands gripped the steering wheel tightly as I tried my hardest not to speed on my way home. It was funny how just a week ago I didn't want to go home and now I couldn't get there fast enough.

When I pulled up into my driveway I let out a small breath when I noticed that both of my parent's cars were there- although that still didn't stop me from running up the asphalt to the front door when I didn't hear the sound of their voices yelling. My bag was slung loosely over my shoulder and I let it slide off and on to the floor the minute I stepped foot into my house.

I opened my mouth to call out to my parents but immediately snapped it shut when I saw the suitcases next to the front door, thrown on top of each other like the person who had placed them there had been in a rush.

"Mum?" I croaked hesitantly, already feeling tears prick at my eyes. "Dad?"

"Oh, hi honey. It's good to see you." My mum said, walking into the front foyer from the kitchen. Her eyes were red and her face was slightly blotchy, like she had been crying.

"Where's Dad?"

"Up here, darling." I looked up and saw my dad standing on the top of the stairs, another suitcase in his hand. That made four suitcases, four suitcases. My dad barely owned any clothes- he figured he only needed enough to make it to the next laundry day- so I couldn't imagine what he could possibly fit in four suitcases.

"Where are you going, Dad?"

He had his signature smile on his face as he came bounding down the stairs, throwing the suitcase on to the pile with the rest of them. "On a business trip, to California."

"For how long?" I asked hesitantly, afraid to know the answer. My Dad only took a duffle bag when he went on business trips, and those were for a week. I couldn't bear to imagine how long he was going if he had this much luggage.

"Ah," He shrugged, running his hand through his mop of un-tamed brown hair, "We'll see. In the meantime, give me a hug, my pretty girl." Dad tightened his arms around me, I could barely breathe but I didn't want to tell him that- not when I had this horrible feeling that I wouldn't be seeing him for a little while. "I'm going to miss you, Zoe." He lacked his normal enthusiasm when he said this, and for a minute he sounded like the broken man he had been in the weeks following Mark's death. When he pulled away his smile had returned.

My dad was gone not twenty minutes later, I watched from the front porch- my hands shaking- as he drove down the street, not once glancing back.

"He's not going on a business trip is he?" I asked my mum, who had her arm wrapped hesitantly around me.

"Oh, honey." She broke down, tears streaming down her cheeks. Mum pulled me into her chest and we held each other and cried- for Marcus, for Dad, for our ruined relationship- until there were no more tears.

CHAPTER 9

The tension was plausible in the kitchen that morning. The only sound that filled the room was Mum scraping the residue of her breakfast off the pan and into the garbage bin.

We were careful not to make eye contact as we each ate our respective breakfasts, neither of us daring to bring up my Dad's departure or our night spent crying in each other's arms.

When I woke up this morning I was alone on the couch with a blanket covering me. It wasn't until twenty minutes later that my mum came down the stairs. She seemed hesitant to say anything; opening and closing her mouth a few times before she turned away from me and walked into the kitchen.

Now we were here, myself with a bowl of cereal and Mum with some french toast. The bags under my eyes felt heavy and my eyes felt incredibly dry- from all of that crying, I thought dryly. Watching as Mum stood from the table and made a move to the sink to wash her soiled dish.

"I-" Mum paused, her hands still in the sink with her back towards me, "I'm going to head to work now. I'll see you later."

She quickly wiped her hands on the towel next to the sink, still not daring to look at me. I knew my mother, and I knew that she was probably embarrassed. She had always had the perfect life that all of her friends had envied, and now her son was dead, her daughter was lifeless, and her husband had left her.

She stopped at the doorway and turned around to face me, "I love you, darling." Not a moment later she was gone, leaving me with my bowl of cereal.

"Do you mind if I sit here?"

I took my eyes of my questionable cafeteria lunched and noticed Maria standing before me, hovering uncertainly before an empty chair at my table. I gave her the brightest smile that I could muster and motioned for her to sit.

"How are you?" Maria asked, her hands expertly unwrapping the plastic wrap off of her tuna sandwich.

Instead of telling her how I felt like I was going to cry at any moment and what happened with my parents the night before, I settled on a shrug. "You?" I asked, trying to change the topic.

"Oh, well; today in art my teacher actually told me-"

She didn't have a chance to finish her story, as we were interrupted by a man with a very familiar voice. "Is this seat taken?"

I looked up and saw Carter pointing to the seat next to me. I didn't have the patience to deal with him, not now; but I still shook my head.

"Hi, I'm Carter-" He reached across the table after sitting and held his hand out towards Maria, "And you are?"

"Maria." She gave him a friendly smile. When he wasn't looking she turned towards me and raised her eyebrows in a questioning manner. I rolled my eyes and shook my head; trying to tell her that he was not the god that he seemed to be. Although I doubt she caught what I was throwing.

"Why are you here?" I asked bluntly, swiveling in my seat to face Carter. "You never eat in the cafeteria."

He cocked his head to the side, looking at me with that look, "How do you know where I eat?"

"Carter." I warned, narrowing my eyes at him. I really did not have the patience for this right now.

"My friends forgot to wait for me, so I settled on just eating here instead."

I didn't like his answer; I knew that they would never forget to wait for Carter- but I knew that no matter how much I pushed Carter would not change his story. And in that moment I didn't have the energy to even attempt to push him.

"So," Carter turned away from me and looked back to Maria, "tell me about yourself."

The next hour flew by with light conversation and many laughs; and for that hour I was able to forget that my dad was gone and that the boy sitting next to me was the reason that my brother wasn't. Instead, for that hour, the Zoe sitting at the table in the cafeteria resembled the old Zoe.

A few minutes before the bell was scheduled to ring, I said my goodbyes. As I was walking out of the cafeteria, my eyes drifted towards the windows that led to the field. I would have kept walking by them had I not noticed Elli, I paused when I saw her and directed my full attention to the window. It wasn't just Elli eating her lunch on the field, it was Elli, Henry, Jack, and all of Carter's close friends.

I turned to look back towards the table where we had just been eating, noticing that he had already left- probably through the cafeteria door on the other side. I wasn't concerned about that though, instead I was wondering why he would lie to me. Why he would say that his friends had gone out without him, when they hadn't even left school property.

With a frown I turned away from the window, pushed the concern away and went to class.

On my way to my locker after English class my phone started ringing, instantly a light blush came on to my cheeks as my classmates in the hallway all turned to look at me. I frantically began patting my pockets in a search for my phone to stop the loud music from playing. I barely paid the phone number a glance before I held the phone up to my ear, "Hello?" I hissed, assuming that this was one of those telemarketers.

"Hello?" The voice on the other end of the line sounded hesitant, and not like she was trying to sell me something, "Is this Zoe Finley?"

"Yes, it is." I responded, standing off to the side of the hallway so that I was no longer in the way of my classmates who were rushing to get to their own lockers.

"Hi. my name is Sarah Collins, I'm calling from the West Side bookstore."

"Oh!" The application that I had filed a few weeks ago came to mind, "Hi."

"I'm calling to tell you that you got the job; if you'd still like it."

A smile came over my face. Already I could see the pros to the job; the major one being time out of the house and away from my mother. "Of course I'd still like it."

"Great, I'll email you with the details."

I quickly hung up the phone, and navigated my way towards my locker; praying that I wouldn't be late to meet Carter since he was always a stickler for time.

"Where were you?" Carter asked, leaning against his car as he watched me come running towards him.

"I'm early."

"On time." He corrected, pointing to his phone which read 2:35- the time that we had promised to meet to go to his house to work on the project.

"But I'm not late." I added, tugging on my backpack's strap. "Anyways, I got a call from my new boss if you must know."

"You got a job?" He questioned while motioning for me to get in the car.

"Yes," I told him as I strapped on my seat belt, "at the bookstore."

"Zoe," He drew out my name, pausing to look over his shoulder while he reversed, "Do you really think you should be getting a job?"

Oh God, not him too. "Did you talk to Thea?"

"No- I just know the stress you're under and I don't know Zoe, I don't think that this is good for you."

"You don't know me."

"Zoe," He sighed, running a hand over his eyes in frustration, "Maybe you should wait a little bit before getting a job."

"I didn't ask for your opinion, Carter. So please, just drive."

"Love."

I stopped spinning around in the desk chair when Carter spoke, and instead watched him as he laid back onto his bed- staring at the ceiling.

"Love." I repeated.

Our dreaded theme. We had spent hours mulling over how we were meant to find a sub-theme of what, to us, seemed like a singular theme; never mind apply it to one of our novels and then to a real life situation.

He suddenly shot up in the bed, his hair was standing straight up from the way that he had been laying and I had to stifle a laugh at his clueless expression. "Love isn't simple."

"It isn't." I agreed. At this point I was feeling a little brain dead and even the simplest thoughts were making my head hurt.

"There's our sub-theme." Carter clapped his hands together, a boyish grin spreading across his face.

I frowned, not seeing where he was going with it. "You want our sub-theme to be 'love isn't simple'?"

"No." He shook his head, reaching out and holding my left hand with his. I ignored the sensation I felt from where his skin touched mine and focused on looking anywhere but him- my eyes falling on a stack of CD's next to his bed. If I couldn't think before, I sure as heck couldn't think now.

"Then what?"

He squeezed my hand, his eyes shinning. "Turbulent love, true love. Don't you get it- love isn't easy." Carter's smile slowly slipped off his face as his eyes drifted down to our connected hands. "Our love wasn't easy." He said softly, squeezing my hand again- lightly this time.

At the mention of our failed relationship, I slipped my hand out of his. "Don't talk about that."

"Zoe," He sighed, his eyes loosing their shine, "We can't pretend it didn't happen."

"Why not?" My voice was soft as I tried not to whine.

"We dated for a year."

"Eleven months." I corrected, leaning back into the chair. I had spent a lot of time curled up in this chair- watching as Carter did his homework, played video games- or even sometimes watching him as he watched me.

"Close enough."

"So what," I dared to look back at Carter, lifting my gaze from my toes, "Do you want our real-life example to be our relationship?"

"No, we can go out- interview people, ask them about their experiences with love."

I grabbed a pencil from his desk and wrote down the two categories that he had mentioned, wondering if his idea was actually going to work. If I could only ignore the faint feeling of discomfort I could say that we had made a break-through.

"And these categories were in both of the books that we read," Carter commented, standing next to me and leaning over my shoulder to see what I was writing, "I think that this could work, Zoe."

It could, I agreed internally, writing down a few of my own ideas and making sure that what we had corresponded with everything on our rubric. Even as we fell into a comfortable silence, each of us doing our own research and preparations- there was still the elephant in the room of our past relationship.

We had begun dating when we were fifteen, right up until six months before Mark's death. I had been the one to break up with him; my brother had sort of twisted my arm to do it, insisting that Carter and I weren't compatible and that the relationship would never work. Although, looking back now I know that my brother had made me do it because he was jealous that I had been spending more time with his friend than he had.

"I've missed you, Zoe." Carter whispered, when I turned back to look at him an unknown emotion came over his face.

"Carter," My voice cracked slightly as I continued to stare into his eyes, "Don't do this to me." Just because we shouldn't have broken up before, did not mean that we should be getting back together now. Especially not after what he did to my brother.

He nodded, the look on his face passing and instead his signature impassive look replaced it. "You should get going." His voice was cold, nothing like the Carter that had been talking to me before. I knew that this was just one of his defense mechanisms though, and I had learned over the years not to take it personally.

So, I quickly gathered up my things and left- letting Carter drive me home. It felt like we had crossed a bridge that night, the tension between us settling- even if it was just for a moment- but just like that, the tension had returned.

One step forward, two steps back.

CHAPTER 10

There was a Sunday morning tradition in the Finley household. It used to include my entire family; my brother, Mum, Dad and myself. But today, it was just me.

The tradition had started years ago, long before I was born. My parent's used to spend Sunday mornings watching cartoons and eating cereal until nearly noon early in their relationship; the tradition continued after me my brother and I were born, up until his death.

None of us had brought up the tradition again following his death; thinking back on it now, I don't know why we didn't continue it. I suppose that to my parent's it would have been another stark reminder that their son was gone.

I tucked the wool blanket further around myself and settled in to the couch, removing my arm from under the blanket to flip through the channels on the television before settling on a children's channel that was showing reruns of Spongebob Squarepants.

My eyes glazed over as Spongebob came onto the screen, muttering something about Gary. Instead of focusing on the television my mind drifted back to Carter and what he had said to me yesterday.

I've missed you, Zoe.

I blew a piece of hair out of my face in frustration, wondering why he had the right to throw that in my face so easily.

He had been sweet when were dating, the perfect gentleman. But he had never said things like that to me before; things that raised goosebumps on my arms and caused my stomach to flip.

The jarring sound of my phone ringing drew me out of my daze and I looked around for it, tossing the blanket off to the side. When I found it I quickly pressed talk and raised the phone to my ear, "Hello?"

"Zoe? Is this still the right number?"

I frowned, reaching for the remote to mute the television. "Um, yeah. It's Zoe."

"Oh, great! It's Thea."

I sat back on the couch and pulled the blanket over myself again. "Hey, what's up?"

My mind ran as I thought of possibilities as to why Thea would be calling right now, she had rarely called me when Mark was still alive and hadn't called me once since he had died.

"I just wanted to talk to you about what I said the other day."

The other day? I thought back to the last time that I had seen her at the coffee shop, when she had been persistent that I shouldn't get a job. "Oh," I paused, remembering how hurt I had been by the conversation, "What about it?"

"I shouldn't have said that to you and I just wanted to apologize."

A smile fell over my face at how polite Thea was. Even when Mark had first brought her home, I thought that she had been too polite and that it had to be an act- I think that I was coming to realization now that it wasn't an act, mostly because I knew that she had no one to impress anymore. "You don't have to apologize."

"It's just," This time there was a pause on her end and then the sound of a door shutting, "I don't know, Zoe. Getting a job is what helped me to heal but I don't think that's what's going to help you."

She didn't get it, I thought, tugging at a loose thread on the blanket. She just didn't understand how desperately I wanted to heal, I needed to heal. And if working helped Thea to distract herself I don't see why it couldn't help me. "Why not, Thea? How could working possibly hurt me?"

"You're fragile-"

"I am not fragile." I snapped, my grip on the phone tightening. "Don't you dare try and call me weak."

"I'm not calling you weak."

"Fragile and weak are interchangeable."

"That's not what I was trying to say. I know you, Zoe. And I know that being surrounded by people consistently won't make you any happier, you're the kind of person that needs one on one to heal."

I sighed when I finally understood where she was coming from. "I get that now, Thea but- well, I already got a job."

"Oh!" Then another, "Oh... Where?"

"The bookstore, next to the cafe."

"Well-" The sound of my doorbell ringing cut her off, my head snapped to the front foyer wondering who would possibly be at my house before ten on a Sunday morning. "I'll call you later, Zoe." Thea said, disconnecting the call after I said goodbye.

The doorbell rang again before I could get up off of the couch, groaning I made my way to the front door hoping that there wouldn't be a child trying to sell me cookies.

"I don't want-" I started while opening the door but stopped when I noticed it wasn't a child at my front door but instead it was Elli. "What are you doing here?"

"I wanted to come talk to you."

"Me?" I quickly looked over my shoulder to make sure that it was me that she was talking about. It had been months since Elli had been to my house and I don't know what would make today any different. "But why?"

"Well," She stopped and looked over my shoulder, "Is anyone home right now?"

"No." My mum had left in a hurry that morning when she saw me watching cartoons- mumbling an excuse about groceries- and with my dad gone, it was just me.

"Then would you mind if I came in for a few minutes?"

I threw another glance over my shoulder at the mess of blankets I had created on the couch and the three boxes opened cereal on the kitchen counter followed with a glance at my pyjamas. I, nor my house, was in no suitable shape to be accepting visitors. But this was Elli, who was once my best friend- the same girl who had seen me at my highs and lows. I'm sure that she wouldn't care about the state of my house or myself. "Sure," I finally relented, opening the door wider so that she could walk in, "come on in."

A few minutes later Elli stood awkwardly in front of the kitchen counter, myself behind it. I watched her warily; wondering if she had come here to tear my head off or if she just wanted to talk. For my own sake I hoped that it was the latter. "Can I ask you something?"

"Of course." Her shoulders relaxed slightly when I broke the silence and a hesitant smile graced her face.

"Why did you give me that book?"

Her eyebrows pulled together slightly but I wasn't buying her confused look, I knew that she had given it to me because she thought that I had depression. Which, I guarantee, I did not.

"Don't you know?"

I shook my head, confused as to what she was talking about.

"I wanted to show you that there was an alternative, that you could be happy."

"But that's not what the book is about." I protested, my hands gripping the kitchen counter tightly when it began to dawn on me that the entire plot of a book would not be revealed in the first few pages.

"Did you read the entire thing?"

I shook my head again suddenly feeling incredibly guilty. The entire world wasn't against me; Elli wasn't against me.

"Promise me you'll read it." She offered, tucking a strand of hair behind her ear only to have it slip out because of the short length of her hair.

"Of course." I murmured before I let go of the kitchen counter completely. "Would you like something to eat?"

She bit her lip as she looked at my hand resting on the handle of the fridge door. "No, I'll be quick."

My hand fell limp at my side before I motioned for her to sit at the table behind her. We each took a seat, the chair legs scraping against the cold tile floor when we did. I didn't know what to say to her; what could you possibly say to someone who you hadn't had a normal conversation with for five months. Slowly I came to realize that this was her time to talk, not mine.

"I'm sorry." She said finally, her doe eyes meeting mine. I could tell by the look in her eyes that the apology was sincere.

"For what?"

"Not being there for you." With that Elli's eyes drifted down to the table as if she were ashamed with what she had done.

"Why weren't you there for me?" I asked, my voice cracking in the middle of the sentence. Part of me didn't want to hear the answer- I didn't want to hear why none of my friends would come within ten feet of me after my brother passed away. It was almost as if they thought that I was the reason for his death.

She twisted her lips. "I thought you needed space."

I cocked my head to the side, my eyebrows knitting together. She thought that I needed space? Space was the last thing that I needed after my brother's death. All that I truly needed was a shoulder to cry on- a shoulder that I wouldn't get from my mum or dad because they were to busy crying themselves. Instead I turned to my friends for help, but they weren't there. "I needed you."

"I didn't know."

"You should've asked." I countered, feeling tears pricking at the corners of my eyes.

"Oh, Zoe." She sighed, coming around the table to crouch in front of me and wrap her arms around my shoulders. "I'm so sorry."

I didn't answer her, instead I just wrapped my arms around her her and let my tears fall onto her shoulder. This is what I needed five months ago when I was crying alone in my bedroom; I needed someone to hold me as I let the tears fall. Although, it was always better late then never.

Elli left a few hours after that. After I finished shedding the tears that I had been holding in we talked about everything and nothing- dancing around the topics of my parents, my brother, and how much we had changed in the past few months. Instead we talked about Big Brother, who was dating who, and Carter.

She had been the one to bring up Carter, mentioning that he had brought up our project to her. Only Elli and I didn't talk about the project, instead she hammered me with questions about our relationship. I insisted that it was too soon to be dating someone, I wasn't nearly emotionally stable enough to be dating someone- never mind be the person for them to lean on.

Yet she wouldn't let it go.

I got her to drop the topic when I brought up Henry. It only took moments for her eyes to glaze over and the stories of how she developed feelings for him to start spewing out. She didn't bring up Carter again during the rest of her visit.

"I'm home." I heard my mum call out, I looked up from my spot on the couch and saw her drop some grocery bags onto the floor.

"Do you need help?" I asked, already making a move to grab the bags from her.

"No, I only have a few bags."

I crossed my arms and leaned against the wall next to the door as she kicked off her shoes. "It took you nearly five hours to get a few bags?"

Immediately her shoulders fell and a guilty look crossed over her face. "Honey..." She trailed off, already grabbing the bags and making a move to put them in the kitchen. "I needed to get some air."

I shook my head, turning away from her and walking back into the family room. A mother shouldn't have to get air to avoid talking to her daughter.

"Zoe, I just-" She stopped talking when the sound of the phone ringing cut her off, startling us both.

I reached for it but immediately froze when I saw the name on the screen.

Dad.

"Are you going to answer it?" Mum asked softly after seeing the name on the screen.

I wanted to. I really did. I wanted to hear my dad's voice, I wanted to hear him tell me that he was coming home and he truly was on a business trip. But deep down I knew that he would make up more excuses that would leave me feeling deflated when we broke up.

"No."

I needed to move on; and maybe learning who in my life wanted the best for me was the first step. Maybe I was finally learning what moving on was really about.

CHAPTER 11

Marcus Finley.

I ran my finger over his name that was written in the back of the tattered used book I held in my hand.

It was my first day of work, my boss- Sarah- had kept me on the easier jobs; sweeping, putting away books, going to pick up lunch.

And now this. She had asked me to organize that used books that were for sale; the shelf was tucked away in a rarely visited corner at the back of the book store.

When I first laid my eyes on the book I immediately recognized it as one of the books that Marcus had kept shoved in his too-small bookshelf; it still had the same crease right down the middle of the cover.

I used to tease him about the bookshelf. He had refused to buy a new one, saying that the one he currently had worked just fine; when in actuality he could barely pull the books out neverind put them in.

The last time that I had been into his room the books were still there, tucked in to his bookshelf like a jigsaw puzzle. And now they were here- at the bookstore.

I suppose my mum was finally moving on; and for her it involved clearing out my brother's bedroom.

"Zoe?" I whirled around at the sound of Sarah's voice and found her standing behind me, surrounded by the imposing bookshelves. "Is everything okay?"

I bit my lip before flipping the book over in my hand, "I think so."

"Do you need help?" She nodded towards the book, "all you need to do with that one is place a price tag on it then put it on the shelf."

The thought of someone else taking home my brother's book unsettled me. Especially this one, which he had read many, many times. "Actually, I think that I'm going to buy this one."

Sarah shrugged, tugging on her blonde ponytail and grabbing the broom she had left resting on the bookshelf beside her. "Just put it aside and ring it through at the end of your shift then." I watched as she backed away towards the children's section, "Let me know if you need any help!" And then she was gone.

My eyes drifted back towards the book in my hand. I didn't read, the book that my brother was going to give to me as a birthday present had been the first book that I actually successfully read since we were required to read novels in elementary schools- and then there was the book that Elli had given to me. And now this one.

Shaking my head I placed the book off to the side, determined to direct my focus back to the task at hand. I eventually developed a steady rhythm; slap the price tag on, slide it onto the bookshelf- then repeat. I tried to ignore the fact that half of the books in the donated box belonged to my brother. I knew that if I bought them back my mum wouldn't be too happy.

The silence of the bookstore was broken by the jarring sound of the my ring tone, screaming out the theme song from The Big Bang Theory. My cheeks were on fire as I reached for my phone, fumbling to press the talk button to stop the song.

"Yes?" I hissed, peaking behind the bookshelf to make sure that no one was coming to rip my head off.

"Hey! It's Carter."

I frowned, wondering why he was calling. We hadn't agreed to meet up this weekend- I made sure of that when I got my schedule for work. "Am I forgetting something?" I asked, chewing on my bottom lip. I still felt guilty about the time that I had fallen asleep when were meant to be meeting up.

"No I, uh- no." He stammered, "I just wanted to ask, well- would you like to go out for dinner?"

"Dinner?" I squeaked, dropping the box of books that I had just picked up. "Carter- you know that I don't have feelings for you anymore-"

"It's not a date." He cut me off, his voice taking on a cold tone. "We have to start doing the research for our project and I just thought-" Carter paused and I could hear him taking a deep breath, "you know what? Never mind Zoe, I'll talk to you later."

"Wait!" My teeth gripped harder on my bottom lip as I collected myself and slowly came to realize what an idiot I had made of myself. "I'm sorry."

"It's fine." His voice had thawed a little bit and I knew that he wasn't that mad; he just wasn't used to a girl not falling over their feet to get to him. "So, tonight?"

I pulled my phone away from my ear to check the time and saw that I only had half an hour left in my shift. "I'd love to." I confirmed before picking up the box that I had dropped.

"I'll pick you up at six then?" He asked, his voice returned to his normal tone but I could tell that he wasn't back to smiling yet.

After agreeing on the time I hung up, trying to focus again on the task at hand. Instead my mind kept drifting back to what I had said to Carter- did I really not have feelings for him anymore? Deep down I knew that was probably a lie.

Feelings like the ones that I had for Carter didn't go away so quickly. Not when every kiss, touch, or even look from him used to send my stomach into a fit of butterflies- an affect that I'm almost positive that he still had on me.

As I picked up the empty box and started to walk in the direction of the recycling bin I knew that I had lied to Carter; deep down I still loved him.

I used to be the type of girl that would fret over what clothes to wear and what boys thought of my hair. But now I was more concerned if I would be able to make it through the day without breaking down in tears because of him.

Yet here I was, half of my closet lying on the floor around me and I still couldn't find anything to wear. I kicked at the clothes that were covering my feet. I had spent the last few months wearing sweatpants and sweatshirts, and it seemed that in that time I had lost my sense of style and half my nice clothes.

I was about to settle on a pair of jeans and an oversized sweater when my mum came walking in, a black piece of fabric in her hands. She held it up before me and I recognized it as one of my old skirts that I used to wear religiously. "How's this?" She questioned, pushing it forward.

"Wow." I paused, reaching out to grab it from her hands. "Thank you, Mum." I said softly, running my hands over the skirt.

She opened her mouth to answer but was cut off by the doorbell. "That should be him then." She grinned, reaching forward to squeeze my hand before leaving me alone in the bedroom.

A few minutes later I came stumbling down the stairs. It had been a while since I pulled out my wedges but it seemed like now was the perfect time to do so. "Hey." I gave Carter a small smile when I saw him, still unsure if he was upset because of what I said before.

"Hi." Carter said, his voice a notch deeper than normal. His eyes ran up and down my body before he cocked his head out the door, "are you ready to go?"

I said a quick goodbye to mum and followed him down the steps towards his car. The car ride to the restaurant was silent, we both were still unsure as to wear we stood with each other.

Before Mark's death we had been so comfortable together that even when we didn't talk it felt like we were still getting closer. Now, the silence between us felt like we were getting pulled even further apart.

"Are-"

"This-"

We both started talking at the same time out of a desperate need to fill the silence between us. Carter laughed softly, motioning for me to go ahead.

"Are we just going to pick a random couple to interview or..." I trailed off, looking to Carter to fill in the rest. I had been so frazzled on the phone earlier that I didn't even think to ask him wat his plan was.

He shrugged, taking a right turn on a street that lead us deeper into downtown Toronto. "I guess we'll just go with the flow." A moment later he pulled into the parking lot of a small Italian restaurant, the bright sign reading Carisma casting a soft blue glow on the parking lot.

I placed my hand on the door handle, ready to push open the door but Carter was already there- holding out his hand for me to take. "This isn't a-"

"Date." Carter finished for me, squeezing my hand as I climbed out of his car. "I know, I'm just doing the gentlemen thing."

Out of habit I rolled my eyes. As much as Carter wanted the student body to believe that he was a gentlemen, he was the furthest thing from it. Carter had always been the awkward fumbling boy that you took pity on- inside he was still that boy, but he had developed the muscles and good looks that seemed to cover it up.

"M'lady." Carter mocked, holding open the door for me. "After you." He motioned into the restaurant, the international sign for 'go ahead'.

I walked up to the hostess' booth, Carter hovering right behind me. The restaurant was what all Italian restaurants aimed to be. The roof was decorated like the night sky and portraits of the streets of Italy were painted on the wall; for a moment if felt like you were actually in Italy. "This place is gorgeous." I murmured to Carter, not wanting to break the atmosphere.

Carter pointed ahead, where an elderly lady and man were dancing off to the side of the restaurant- they were mostly hidden by shrubs but you could still see them sway back and forth to the soft music playing in the background. "Do you think they work here?" I asked Carter, a smile falling on my lips as the man kissed her forehead.

"Actually," a voice interrupted us and we both spun around to see a women standing before us, "they own the place."

"They seem in love." I commented, watching as the waitress grabbed two menus for us.

"They've been married for nearly fifty years," she told us, peaking back at them dancing with a smile on her face. "I would hope so."

A few moments later we were sat at a table located at the back of the restaurant. I was captivated by the string of lights that hung along the walls, staring at them instead of at my menu. "Where did you find this place?" I asked in awe, wondering how Carter who thought a date to McDonald's was romantic could find something as beautiful as this.

"My mom; she loved it here- she used to drag my dad here nearly every week and I thought I'd see what the rage was all about."

I knew that his mom was a sensitive topic; even a blind man could see that. But for some reason I found myself leaning forward and grabbing his hand in mine, "how is she?"

His eyes drifted away to me to something over my shoulder before he pulled his hand out from under mine. "Hello! I heard you two wanted to talk to us?" I turned around with a smile to see the same couple that we had seen dancing before, now holding hands at the head of our table.

I tried to give Carter a look that said we'll be talking about this later but he refused to make eye contact with me, instead he watched as Patricia and Antonio pulled up two chairs to join us at the table. I did want to talk to him later- even back when we had been dating Carter had spent most of his nights worried about his mother; he had nearly killed himself by forgetting to eat and sleep during the nights he spent at the hospital.

I clamped down on my cheek as I let my eyes trail over him. He had bags under his eyes, but those had been there since the first day that his mother was diagnosed with breast cancer. What really concerned me was that fact that he seemed a bit thinner- had he lost weight? Oh God, I truly hoped that he was still eating.

"Zoe!" My head snapped up at the sound of my name and I saw that all three of them were trying to get my attention.

"Sorry, I must have zoned out." I mumbled, feeling a blush creeping up my neck.

"No problem, dear." Patricia smiled, her blue eyes sparkling. "Your boyfriend was just saying that you had some questions for us?"

"He's not my-" I started to correct her but instead just shook my head, realizing that there was no point in trying to explain our relationship. "How did you two meet?" I asked them instead, picking the first question that I had written in my notebook.

"Back in Italy," Patricia started, her gaze leaving mine to look at her husband, "we were getting on the same ship to come over here and he told me that I was beautiful."

"We weren't on the same ship." Antonio corrected, causing a small frown to come across Patricia's face as she looked up at her husband. "We met over here."

"We met in Italy, darling." Patricia told him, giving me a smile and a shake of her head as if to say 'Men? What are you going to do with them?'

The conversation continued on like that, Carter and I rotated between asking the couple questions- getting to the bottom of how they made it to where they were today. Yet I still couldn't stop my eyes from drifting over to Carter, my concern hitting me in an overwhelming wave each time I looked at him.

"Okay, one last question." Carter told them. The restaurant had closed a few minutes ago but from the way that Patricia and Antonio were comfortably seated they didn't seem in any rush to get rid of us. "What advice would you give to a young couple?"

"Fight for each other." Patricia said instantly, her eyes drifting between Carter and I before they settled on her husband. "So many times we broke up and I swore that I would never get back together with him, but when you love each other you fight- and sometimes I fought for him and he fought for me. Oh yes, you must also know when to fight. One person can't do all the fighting."

Antonio laughed, wrapping his arms around Patricia's shoulders. "Exactly what she said- be persistent. If you truly love someone you will find a way to make it work."

As I watched Carter thank Patricia and Antonio with a wide smile on his face, I couldn't help but wonder why he never fought for me.

CHAPTER 12

My parents had, what they liked to call, Thursday night dates. Without skipping a beat- every Thursday for as long as I could remember they had their dates.

I always used to think that was what made their relationship so perfect but I knew now, that it wasn't what you did so much as the effort that you put in to the relationship.

The date nights were put on an indefinite hold after Mark's death, and I suppose they're on a definite hold now that my dad was gone. That's why I was a little surprised to see my mother in one of her favourite black dresses, hesitantly knocking on my door.

"I have something to ask you." She eyed me warily, watching as I closed the untouched school books that I had opened nearly an hour ago and pushed them off to the side of my bed.

I motioned for her to continue when I realized that she wasn't going to come any further into the room.

"How," she paused for a moment, running a hand through her hair, "how would you feel if I went out?"

"With Dad?" I scoffed. Somewhere over the past two weeks I had come to terms with the fact that my dad and my mum weren't the same people that they were when they got married and that maybe this split was for the best; my mum looked the happiest she had in months.

"Oh- um, no." Her eyes danced around my bedroom in an attempt not to meet my gaze, "you see, this friend of mine from high school is in town and he asked me out to dinner- it's not a date, though! I'm not quite ready for that yet."

"Mum-"

"If you feel uncomfortable at all, just tell me and I won't go."

"Mum-"

"Really darling, just tell me. I know that we aren't on the best of terms but you're still my baby girl and I want to know how you feel about this."

"Mum! Listen to me."

"Oh." Her head shot up and her eyes widened, "Sorry, Zo. Go ahead."

I gave her a small smile, shaking my head at how nervous that she was. I knew that I shouldn't like that she was going out with another man instead of trying to work things out with my dad- but there was no denying that her usual lifeless eyes had a certain spark to them. "I want you to have fun."

This time she shook her head, coming to sit on the edge of my head. "I don't think it'll be that easy."

"Why not?"

She let out a laugh that sounded more like a sigh, "I don't know if I'm ready."

I waited a moment before saying, "you deserve to be happy, Mum."

"Oh Zoe," She gave me a sad smile, running her hand over my hair, "so do you."

My boss was still reluctant to give me harder jobs- especially ones that involved actually talking to customers. But after the two girls that were meant to be manning the cash called in sick, she had no choice but to put me on the floor.

"Just be polite." Sarah told me, watching as I fiddled around with the cash register. She had given me a crash course on it but it still looked like a foreign creature to me.

"I can be polite." I told her, rolling my eyes. I had a sneaky feeling that Elli had told Sarah about my not so nice backstory based on the way Sarah seemed to be on constant pins and needles around me.

"I know you can, I also know that we get pretty rude customers in here on a Saturday and-"

"Sarah, please." I stopped her, spinning around with my hands on my hips. She had been standing very close behind me inspecting my every move, "just go, I'll be fine."

She chewed on her bottom lip for a few moments and I could see the wheels turning in her head. In her position I probably wouldn't want to leave an emotionally unstable teenage girl manning the shop- especially one who had only worked a few shifts. From my position though, this looked like the perfect opportunity to prove that I was capable of actually doing something that required a little thought and independence.

"I can just stay." Sarah said finally, throwing her coat and purse down on to a nearby chair.

I marched over to where her belongings lay and practically shoved them into her arms, "Sarah, you can't miss your sister's baby shower."

"She won't even notice that I'm not there."

"She's your sister, of course she'll notice."

"But, Zoe-"she groaned, her hands hesitantly grabbing her coat and purse from me.

"Go."

"Are you sure you'll be okay?" She continued to chew on her bottom lip, her gaze floating around the shop like she expected it all to collapse before her. "I really don't mind staying to help."

"It's five o'clock on a Saturday, we close in two hours- I'll be fine."

"Okay." She quickly tucked her arms into her coat, securing the buttons before throwing her purse over her shoulder. "But you'll call if you need anything?"

"Of course."

Moments later she was gone, the door closing with a conclusive ding behind her. The minute I saw her figure disappear around the corner I collapsed into one of the chairs behind the cash register, resting my elbows on the counter and placing my forehead in my palms.

I thought that this job would be what I needed, that it would settle down my brain that seemed to never stop moving- but instead all that I seemed to be getting from this experience was more stress. And trust me when I say that I already had more than enough stress.

My thoughts were interrupted by the sound of the bell above the door ringing. I didn't lift my head from my hands, knowing that it was probably just Sarah coming back with another excuse as to why she should stay. "Sarah, seriously- I told you to go and," the speech that I had prepared when died in my mouth when I saw who was standing in front of me.

"Not Sarah," The boy shrugged, tucking his hands in to the pockets of his jeans, "just me."

Oh God, he looked exactly the same.

"Zach."

Oh those eyes, those eyes will haunt me until the day I die.

"How are you, Zoe?"

And his hair; I wonder if he's cut it in the past few months.

I ignored his question, "what are you doing here?"

My gaze flickered down to his lips, those same lips that had formed the words, 'I don't feel the same way anymore, Zo.'

"I wanted to see you." He moved his hair out of his eyes with a simple flick of his head.

"It's been four months."

"Four months too long." He smirked, catching his bottom lip between his teeth.

"You broke up with me." I whispered, my voice betraying me on the last word. Looking into his captivating blue eyes I couldn't help but feel like the same broken girl I had been when I begged him to reconsider, to tell me that he still loved me.

He moved his eyes away from me like it was my fault. "You were broken."

"I wasn't- I broke after that day."

My chest was getting tight and I couldn't breath- seeing this boy in front of me was like seeing a ghost; a very unwelcome ghost.

"I thought that you weren't the same girl that I fell in love, but I realized now that you were- and Zoe I-"

"Don't say it." I warned, my hand flying to my head. This was too much. Too much. "You need to leave."

"And you need to hear this." He took a step closer towards me, holding his hands up in a warning stance.

It was getting hot in here and I couldn't breathe. Not when Zach was standing in front of me; a sudden reminder of the night that Mark died.

Images from that night came flying back to me like a movie that was skipping, each one hitting me with a blow that brought me closer and closer to the ground.

Bam. Me crying on Elli's bedroom floor, wondering why Zach wasn't mine anymore.

Bam. Getting the call from my mum saying that my brother was dead.

Bam. The tears that filled my eyes as I drove to the hospital.

Bam. Struggling against the arms of my father to get to my brother; he couldn't be dead, he just couldn't.

Bam. Breaking through and finding my brother cold and pale and dead.

Then I hit the floor of the bookstore.

I met Zachary Anderson at my school's football game. Elli had a little crush on one of the football players on our team- a crush that only last for another couple of weeks after this day- and had insisted that we go watch their game against our rival school.

It was at the end of November and I had still been dating Carter then. He refused to come to the game, saying that football wasn't 'his scene'. So it was just Elli and I bundled up under the blanket watching the boys run back and forth chasing after the football.

Needless to say, I didn't have the best understanding of football. I had tried to learn for Elli's sake but sitting on the cold bleachers with snow falling down around you wasn't exactly the best place to try and learn a brand new concept.

The game had just ended when he appeared at the bottom of the bleachers, his forehead coated in sweat and a cocky grin on his face. "Ladies." He nodded his head towards us, his eyes glazing over Elli and landing on me. "I couldn't help but notice that you seemed a little lonely."

"Oh, Zoe is but I-"she paused, looking across the field at the boy we had come to watch- the same one that was waving at her like a mad man, "I have someone waiting for me."

I had mouthed 'what the hell?' at her as she ran across the field, leaving me alone with one of the players of the rival team. Elli knew that I had a boyfriend but she had no trouble playing little games like this. I subtly gave her the middle finger when she shrugged at my question before I turned back to the boy in front of me.

"So, Zoe, huh?" He asked, the grin not slipping from his face as I studied him with a frown.

"And you are?"

"Zach." He waited a moment before continuing, "would you like to go on a date with me?"

"Unfortunately I'm accounted for." I looked over at the parking lot and noticed Carter leaning against his car, looking at us with his own frown- I had tried to give him a reassuring smile but I knew that I would be bombarded with questions the minute I entered his car.

Zach had simply shrugged, not seeming fazed by my answer. "Well, if that guy breaks up with you I'll be there."

True to his word, three months later when Carter and I broke up Zach had been there- knocking on my door nearly a week later. I had never found out how he knew where I lived or the fact that Carter and I had broken up; instead I of asking those questions I agreed to go on a date with him.

At first I considered him a rebound; someone that I would date for a couple of months before moving on to a more serious relationship. Yet it didn't take long for me to realize that I was developing feelings for Zachary Anderson and he was developing him for me too.

He was funny, he was cute; he was everything I need.

I had truly loved Zach right up until the day that he broke my heart.

"What did you do to her?"

"Zoe, honey. You need to wake up."

"I did nothing, Jacobs. Back off."

"Then why is she currently unconscious in the back of a bookstore, Anderson?"

"Come on Zoe, you're okay."

"How the hell would I know? I was talking to her and next thing I know she was lying on the floor."

"I'm going to kill you when she wakes up."

"I'd like to see you try."

"Can you all just shut up?" I groaned, I kept my eyes shut as I waited for the steady throbbing to subside.

"Oh thank God, Zoe." I heard Elli say, followed shortly by something cold being pressed to my forehead.

I didn't know where I was but I did know that whatever I was lying on was not comfortable and suddenly I wished that I was lying in my bed. With a lot of effort I opened my eyes, the brightness of the light immediately flooding in which caused the pounding in my skull to multiply.

"What the hell happened?" I groaned, letting Elli hold the ice pack on my forehead. The last thing that I remembered was sitting on the stool and then Zach coming in- Zach.

My head spun around faster than I probably should have considering how much it hurt right now, but I found a blank faced Zach leaning against the doorway to the employee's room of the bookstore.

"You blacked out."

"Because of you." Carter snarled, his fists clenched in a threatening manner at his sides.

"Boys." I grabbed the ice pack from Elli and turned my entire body to face them, the blanket that had been over my shoulders falling to the floor. "You both need to shut up." If they talked any louder I had a feeling that my head was actually going to explode.

"He shouldn't have been here." Carter commented, his fists relaxing slightly when his gaze landed on me curled up on the couch. "He always fucking does this to you."

"What?" Zach scoffed, "I didn't push her."

I could practically feel the anger rolling off of Carter in waves as he turned to Zach, "no, but you still found a way to hurt her."

"Oh lay off, Jacobs. Like you've never hurt her."

"Not physically."

"I didn't push her." Zach nearly growled, his face turning red with anger as he pushed himself up against Carter.

I held my breath as the boys got closer and closer together, each one sending silent threats with the look in their eyes.

"You two need to cut this out." Elli warned them, pushing her way in between them. She was tiny, but she still had the desired effect- the boys pulled apart; each one going to a different side of the staff room.

"Okay, Carter and I are going to take Zoe home- Zach you need to leave." Elli commanded, watching as Carter kicked at the coffee maker and Zach came closer to me. I didn't want him near me, especially not with this overwhelming throbbing coming from my head.

He shook his head, rolling his lips together as he looked between Carter and Elli before they settled on me, "I'm sorry, Zoe; for everything." Zach pushed past Carter and out of the staff room, leaving behind an air of confusion.

"What was he doing here?" Carter asked me, pointing to where Zach had just left. "You two broke up."

"Leave her alone, Carter-" Elli warned him, noticing the desperate look on my face, "I'm going to take her home now, you can either leave or wait here for me to come back."

He shook his head looking between me and the door before settling on the exit, "whatever, I'm leaving." He slammed the door to the staff room shut behind him, the sound of his heavy footsteps and then the shop door closing following.

"I thought you said you both were going to drive me home?" I asked softly, pushing the ice pack harder against my head in hopes that it would dull the pain a little faster.

Elli gave me a sad look, "he's angry- he needs time to cool off."

"Oh Elli," I groaned, my head falling back against the couch when I realized what a mess I made of my first day taking care of the shop on my own, "I can't do anything right, can I?"

She laughed, sitting on the couch next to me and pulling my closer to her, "don't worry, Zo. We'll figure it out."

I leaned my head on her shoulder, looking at the bookshelf across from us. As I sat there silently in the room with Elli, trying to gather my thoughts, I couldn't help but be grateful that no matter how many times I tried to push her away- Elli still came when I needed her.

CHapTer 13

Acceptance.

I've always had a hard time trying to grasp this concept.

After I broke up with my first boyfriend I had cried for a week straight, binging on ice cream and silly love movies. Granted, I was only thirteen and I know that I shouldn't have taken it that hard- especially when I still had a life filled with pointless relationships and awkward kisses to look forward to; but for some reason in that moment that one break up felt like the end of the world.

When I finally crawled out from under my blankets it took me a while to realize that I no longer had a boyfriend; no one to kiss or send silly text messages too.

It was absolutely brutal to watch all of my friends walk through the hallways with their boyfriends, holding hands and looking so happy- although I would bet money that all the couples that I was so envious of have probably broken up now.

Once I finally did come to terms with the fact that I was the single friend, I had a whole other things to learn to accept- my ex-boyfriend dating someone else. That took another two weeks of tears and more than a few tubs of ice cream before I was ready to face him again.

I was still learning to accept the fact that I was an only child now. It was hard to go from, 'Oh, you're Mark's sister' when people learned my name to 'I heard about your brother, I'm so sorry for your loss'. It was even harder to walk by his bedroom door, knowing that it would be eternally shut.

And sometimes, for the first few seconds after I wake up, I can almost pretend that Mark is still alive. That he is fast asleep in his bed, late to wake up for school as always. It wouldn't take long for the realization to set in that my brother was not going to wake up- that he wasn't asleep in his bed and then the reality of my life would hit me like a slap to my face.

Needless to say I wasn't good with acceptance. I still hadn't accepted the fact the fact that my brother was dead- sometimes I closed my eyes when I heard the doorbell ring and wish for a few seconds that it was my brother standing behind the door telling me that his death, his funeral, everything was all a prank. Only it was never hi.

Even if I wasn't ready to accept the fact that Mark wasn't coming back, life went ahead and hit me with a brand new thing that I had to learn to come to terms with- the harsh reality that my parent's relationship was done.

I realize now that they probably weren't going to get back to- gether, but that still doesn't make it any easier to deal with. Mostly because with my parent's being separated it made Mark's death so much more real.

It reminded me that my life wasn't the same- that my perfect family wasn't, well, perfect.

Yet I still couldn't help but sit on my mother's bed- watching as she tried on different dresses to get ready for her first date with a man that wasn't my dad.

Mum twirled around in front of her floor length mirror in a red sundress, she slipped on a pair of black flats and turned around for my opinion- her hands on her hips as she waited.

"Too casual." I murmured, cocking my head towards her closet- this was my signal for 'next one' which had been created after the first five dresses that she had put on.

Our little routine carried on for another thirty minutes before the doorbell rang and my mother stood in front of me wearing nothing more than a very shocked expression.

"I wasn't expecting him for another twenty minutes." She choked out, looking around her room at the mess of clothes on her door. "Oh my God Zoe, what am I going to do?"

I pushed away the urge to laugh at my mother who looked like a teenage girl getting ready on her prom night. I reached forward and grabbed a black dress that Mum had looked stunning in and tossed it to her just as the doorbell rang for a second time. "I'll get the door," I told her, nodding towards the dress that she now held in her hands, "and you better wear that or I'm going to send him home."

I left her bedroom to go answer the door, the sound of my mother's laughter following me down the hallway.

I leaned against my headboard, a bowl of ice cream in my lap. It had been two hours since my mum had left and I couldn't help but feel a little like her mother; eagerly waiting for her to come home.

I had mixed feelings about the date. Part of me hoped that it went well; I genuinely liked seeing a smile on my mum's face but another part of me really wished that the guy was a complete jerk and Mum would realize that she didn't need a man.

Although, judging by the few words that I had shared with this guy- Ken- I could tell that he was a nice guy. He even brought flowers for my mum, saying that the blue matched her eyes. I had faked a gag at this and practically pushed them out of the house, not missing the light blush that fell on Mum's cheeks when she met Ken's eyes.

I blew a piece of hair out of my face at the same moment that a beeping sound emitted from my cellphone. I frowned, unplugging my phone and bringing it closer to me.

8:47pm

From: Carter

I'm sorry.

My frown deepened as I stared at the message. I wanted to think that I was still mad at him, but I knew that I wasn't. That was just Carter- over protective and very short tempered. It was one of the many things that made CarterCarter.

8:47pm

From: Carter

zoe, please. I shouldn't have acted like that

8:48pm

From: Carter

answer me zo

My fingers hovered over the keyboard, dancing over the keys as I figured out what to send back to him. As I typed, deleted, and re-typed a message Carter proceeded to send me a bunch of emoji's- ranging from the sad face to the dancing lady. I laughed as each emoji appeared on my screen, followed by an apology from Carter.

This was the real Carter- the Carter at school was all a front that he had developed after he was first labelled a 'popular'. This Carter, the one who had just sent me the poop face emoji, was the Carter that I had fallen in love with.

This was my Carter.

8:51pm
From: Zoe
youre spamming my notifications
8:51pm
From: Zoe
please stop
8:52pm
From: Carter
hiiiii zooooeeeee

I rolled my eyes at this message, laughing as he followed it with the blushing face emoji. I think that Carter was the only guy who could make a girl double over in laughter from such simple text messages.

8:52pm
From: Zoe
hi carter
8:53pm
From: Carter
did you see what I said earlier?
8:53pm
From: Zoe
hmm nope? What's that?
8:53pm
From: Carter
Come on Zo
8:54pm
From: Zoe
*zoe to you
8:54pm
From: Zoe
but I forgive you.

8:55pm

From: Zoe

just remember that you dont have to save me all the time carter, im not your responsibility.

I chewed anxiously on my bottom lip wondering how Carter would respond to that message. I didn't know how else to say it to him- but it was true. I wasn't his responsibility; I wasn't anybody's responsibility.

The other day I didn't need Carter to protect me from Zach- that was just Carter's stupid hero complex poking through. He had said something like 'you broke up' to Zach the other night in that accusatory tone of his and it was almost like Carter forgot that we had broken up too.

8:56pm

From: Carter

I've missed you Zoe

8:56pm

From: Carter

and I promised that I would take care of you and I will so suck it up

I spooned another bite of my ice cream into my mouth, rereading his words over and over again until I had memorized them to heart.

Who?

Who had he promised? Not, Mark- they said that he had died on impact.

Unless... Unless my parent's had lied to me.

8:57pm

From: Zoe

Promised who?

8:58pm

From: Carter

Doesn't matter

8:59pm

From: Zoe

It does

9:01pm

From: Carter

Just let it go zo, maybe another day.. just be happy that you have such a stud to protect you

9:01pm

From: Carter

So what's up?

I let the obvious subject change drop, answering his question instantly and quickly our banter turned into a full-fledged conversation and it wasn't long before I realized that we had been talking for nearly two hours.

"Hi, darling."

I looked up to see my mum standing in my doorway, her purse handing limply in her hand.

11:17pm

From: Zoe

I've got to go, mums home

11:17pm

From: Zoe

See you at school?

11:17pm

From: Carter

I'll see you tomorrow :-)

I had to bite down on my bottom lip to keep myself from smiling as I shut off my phone, plugging it back in and putting my now empty ice cream bowl on my bed side table.

"How was your date?" I asked Mum, watching her sit on the edge of my bed and proceed to take off her blue high heels.

"It was good." She said softly, placing her heels beside my bed and crawling over to lay next to me. "Did you like him?"

I shrugged, the question causing my stomach to flip a little bit. Did I? I liked the flowers, I liked his cheesy jokes- but was I ready for him to replace my Dad? No. Was I ready for anyone to replace my Dad? No. "I liked him," I said slowly, playing with the edge of my pillow case, "but I don't think I like the idea of him."

Mum nodded with a sigh, "I know darling. Your Dad and I haven't finalized anything and I just thought that I would try it out," she placed her hand over mine and gave it a little squeeze, "but I don't think I'm quite ready to starting dating seriously again."

I let out a small breath that I hadn't realized I had been holding-feeling totally relieved. Was that bad? I had thought that I was ready for my mum to see someone else but now, I don't think that I was fully ready to spend nights alone with just my mum- never mind adding another man to the mix.

Mum said goodbye a few moments later- giving me a kiss on the top of my head before grabbing her heels and shutting my door; encasing me in darkness.

Out of instinct I reached blindly for my phone to check the time. As I unlocked the screen I was greeted by the notification of a new message.

11:31pm

From: Carter

Goodnight, sleep well zo

This time I couldn't help but let my lips stretch in to a smile.

CHAPTER 14

I used to believe that love was cut and dry. You laid eyes on the man of your dreams, he smiled, you smiled- and that was it, you had found the love of your life.

When I was five I laid eyes on Carter Jacobs and if you had asked me later that day I would have sworn that Carter was my one true love. A few years later the rumour started flying that boys had cooties and Carter suddenly became very unattractive. Eventually I came to view Carter as nothing more than a platonic figure in my life, until I noticed the smile.

We were twelve when I first saw Carter use the smile; he slightly pulled up the edges of his lips- not showing any teeth- and give you a look that made any girls knees go week.

I watched with a smile of my own each time that Carter used that smile on an unsuspecting girls, throwing in a pick-up line to go with it.

I had honestly thought that I didn't have a crush on Carter Jacobs until I started getting jealous each time I saw him use the smile on any other girl but me. It was a jealousy that made my hands curl into fists and my stomach to knot. It was absolutely painful.

Then there was the brief period where that smile was all mine, when I was the only one that he looked at like that.

I had seen the smile since we broke up, not until today- when he stood leaning against the locker next to my own with that stupid, knee weakening smile on his face.

I walked up to my locker, my hands shaking slightly as I fiddled with my Dudley lock.

"Hi." Carter said quietly, bending his knees a fraction so that we were the same height.

I ran my tongue over my lip, keeping my eyes on my lock. What was my combination again?

"Don't do that." Carter said in a hoarse voice, his eyes narrowing in on my lips.

30-21-06? "Don't do what?" I asked, my eyes darting back down to my lock as I bit my lip in concentration.

"That." He touched his finger to my lip and immediately my hand let my lock drop and hit my locker with a loud bang. He ran his calloused finger along the length of my lip and tugged on it slightly, when my teeth were hidden behind my lips he let his hand drop.

My hand flew up to my lip- touching where Carter had touched just moments before. Slowly I caught my breath, raising my eyes to find him looking right back at me. "Carter..."

He ran a hand down his face before letting it fall to his side, "I'm sorry, Zo. I just wanted to, shit-"he tugged on the ends of his hair, his eyes dancing between the students mingling in the hallway and back to me, "I just wanted to ask you about tonight."

"Tonight?" I let my gaze fall back down to my lock, ignoring the fact that the trembling in my hands had intensified.

"Want to go the mall? To do more interviews?"

I nodded, my hands still fiddling with the knob on my lock trying to remember my combination. The last thing that I wanted to do was to spend the night with Carter after the scene that had just happened, but I knew that the project was more important than the fact that I couldn't keep my hands still.

"Alright- I'll text you after class." Carter tapped his hand against my locker one time before turning on his heel and leaving my alone.

I let out my breath that I hadn't realized that I had been holding, letting my shoulders fall. With the absence of Carter my hands finally found remembered my combination.

21-06-30.

Minutes after the bell rang I found myself resting against the wall of the school. It was cold enough for me to have a coat but- even though Christmas break was a few weeks away- there was still no snow.

I used to crave the first snowfall each year, waiting patiently at the window after the weatherman had said that it was coming. Yet this year I couldn't help but hope that there would be no snow- because this would be my first snowfall without my brother and I didn't think that I was ready for that quite just yet.

"Zoe?"

I turned around the find Maria standing next to me, a small smile on her face, "Hey, Maria."

"What's wrong?" She cocked her head to the side as she inspected my face.

"Can't you see that she's clearly upset?" Elli cut in, walking over to stand next to me and across from Maria. "She's crying for goodness sakes."

My hands flew up to touch my cheeks and sure enough when I pulled them away they were damp. "I'm fine." I said softly, cautiously looking between Elli and Maria. As far as I knew my two friends had yet to meet.

"Well, I'm sorry that I wanted to be a little sensitive." Maria snapped, taking a step towards Elli.

Elli rolled her eyes in response, "It's okay, it's obvious that I know her better."

Maria scoffed, raising her hands in a questioning way and nearly hitting a student who had just come walking out of the school doors. "Then where have you been?"

"Girls-"I cut in hesitantly, not knowing what I was supposed to do.

"Well I'm here now," Elli snapped back, "so you're no longer needed."

"Girls, you both need to leave." They each turned to look at me with equal expressions of confusion and shock. "I love you both but right now you both just need to shut up and give me some space."

With a look between each other Elli and Maria both quietly turned around and started walking away, leaving me alone in front of the school.

"Are you going to hop in or are you going to just stand there all day?" My head snapped up at the sound of Carter's voice, pulling me out of my thoughts of Elli and Maria who were now walking in two different directions away from the school.

"I'm coming." I gave him a half-hearted smile and got into his car.

"Are you okay?" I turned to meet Carter's gaze as he spoke, "You look like you've been dragged through hell and back."

I sighed, my gaze drifting out the side window. "I just need a minute, I'll be fine."

"We're not here to shop Carter."

He frowned at my words, his hands putting back the shirt that he had just picked up. "But why can't we multitask?"

"Because I know you," I told him, wrapping my hand around his wrist and tugging him towards the exit of the store that we were currently in, "and multitasking is not in your vocabulary."

It was true, Carter was a single-minded person. If you so much as gave him a sandwich while he was watching TV he wouldn't be able to eat the sandwich until the show was done.

He twisted his lips and shrugged, letting me pull him towards the food court. The mall that we were at was not a large one, but it still had the basic stores that attracted a large variety of people.

"So," I started as we stood at the entrance of the food court, watching as people bustled from the fast food places back to their tables, "who should we interview this time?"

"I think that we should talk to them." He pointed towards a young couple, holding hands and giggling at a table all to themselves towards the front of the food court.

I nodded, watching as the guy fed her a fry. It was obvious that they hadn't been together for too long from the way that they were acting, but I knew that they would probably be willing to answer our questions.

Carter and I stopped at the edge of their table and waited for the kids to stop kissing and look up at us. I played with a loose thread on my shirt, the knowledge that Carter was standing next to be suddenly making me incredibly uncomfortable. Finally Carter cleared his throat which caused them to spring apart almost instantly.

The girl blushed as she looked between the two of us and the guy just wrapped his arm around her, appraising us with a cool glance, "can we help you?" He asked, his eyes still looking between Carter and I.

"We wanted to know if you guys wouldn't mind answering some questions." Carter answered, stepping a little closer to me.

The girl- whose blush was starting to fade- gave Carter a wide smile, "of course we will! Right, Johnny?"

The boy, Johnny, casted his girlfriend a disapproving glance. "I don't know Amanda, we don't know these people."

Amanda shook her head and turned towards us, "Just take a seat."

Not ten minutes later, after discovering the specifics of how the met- at school- and how old they are- fourteen, Carter started to ask the deeper questions which would reflect on to our project.

"What first attracted you to each other?" Carter asked, looking between the couple.

"Well, he is attractive." Amanda giggled, squeezing Johnny's hand in her own. "But I think it was the day that I caught him helping up this poor girl in a lower grade who had tripped down the stairs. All of his friends had laughed at her and left but he stayed behind to help her up."

"I don't know when I first realized that I liked her," Johnny started, his gaze resting solely on Amanda, "one day she was just there and I knew that I was a goner."

Carter and I both laughed at that, writing down exactly what they had both said. "Okay, what advice do you have for other couples?" I asked.

"Don't abandon your friends the minute that you're in a relationship, make sure that you spend equal time with your friends and your boyfriend." Amanda offered, spreading her hands wide on the table as she spoke.

"And for the guys- when she's on her period, don't be afraid. She's the same girl. Plus, if you are afraid of her she probably will get even madder at you than she already is."

Carter laughed at this, reaching forward to high five Johnny while both Amanda and I shot them dirty looks. Within a few seconds we all settled back into a comfortable silence, waiting for Carter to finish writing down what Johnny had said. The sound of Carter's pen scratching stopped and I looked over to him to say the next question, but what I saw made me stop cold.

Carter was already halfway out of his seat with his eyes narrowed in on his target- Zach. He was sitting across the food court, his elbows wresting on the edge of the chair that he was sitting on with his gaze set on us.

"Carter." I warned, reaching out to grab his hand but he pulled it away from me. In a panic I gathered all of our things and shoved them into my purse, muttering a quick apology to Johnny and Amanda before I shot off after Carter who already had Zach held up in front of him by his collar.

"-looking at her?" I caught the tail end of his sentence to Zach, whose face was turning alarmingly red by the second.

"It's a free country." Zach choked out, his feet dangling helplessly in the air.

"Carter, he wasn't doing anything." I tried resting my hand on his arm to get him to settle down but he shook me off, not even glancing in my direction. Cautiously I glanced around the food court, hoping that someone would notice and come and help but at the same time also hoping that no one would notice so that we wouldn't get in trouble.

"See, the girl wants you to let me go." Zach grinned, his hands reaching for Carter's that still held him up by his shirt collar.

"Did you not see the way that he was looking at you?" Carter growled, his eyes still trained on Zach.

"Please Carter, put him down."

But there was no deterring Carter at this point; Zach barely had the chance to blink before Carter threw the first punch.

CHAPTER 15

I had only been to a hospital twice in my life. The first time was after a particularly nasty bicycle accident; I was seven, and it was one of my first times riding a two wheeled bicycle by myself.

At the end of my street was this incredibly steep hill that was 'off-limits' to me when I was seven, and at the bottom of the hill was an imposing metal mail box that was twice the size of my seven year old frame. My mum had gone inside for a few seconds to answer the phone- she made me promise to stay in front of our house on my bike, but my brother had dared me to go down the hill.

So I did.

I was okay at first, peddling down the hill- but in only a few seconds the wheels had begun moving on their own accord and I couldn't control them. All that I remember was staring at the mail box as I got closer and closer to it before I found myself flying over the handle bars of my bike and straight into the large metal box.

That was the first time that I had been to the hospital, the second time being when my brother had died. Yet, for some reason, I still knew exactly how the hospital smelt.

It was this odd smell that could only be labelled as 'hospital'.

I was smelling it now, standing at the edge of the ambulance outside of the mall- looking at my battered ex-boyfriend who was being tended to by the paramedics.

"He provoked me." I could hear Carter talking to the mall's security behind me, I knew that he was looking in my direction- I could practically feel his gaze burning into my back- but I didn't dare turn around.

"Are sure that you're okay?" I asked Zach again, watching as the paramedic motioned for him to lay down on the stretcher.

Zach grimaced as the paramedic applied some anesthetic to the cuts on his cheek, "I'll live," he croaked out.

"Oh, Zach." I sighed, closing my eyes and wondering how I ended up standing at the back of an ambulance from interviewing a couple of kids with Carter. "I'm so sorry."

"S'not your fault."

The paramedic interrupted our strained conversation, asking Zach a series of questions as he twisted Zach's elbow.

"Can I borrow you for a minute?" I heard Carter ask from behind me, obviously done with his own set of questions. I turned around, looking between him and Zach before nodding towards a small bench in front of the mall.

"Only for a minute." I said softly, not knowing how I was supposed to be acting towards him. To be quite frank, I was tired of being hostile but at the same time, I wasn't ready to be friends.

Carter and I sat silently on the bench, each of us staring at the ambulance. People entering the mall walked by it with questioning gazes, obviously wondering why such a badly bruised teenage boy was sitting in the back.

"I'm not going to apologize."

I sighed, keeping my eyes trained ahead, "I didn't expect you to."

"Then I don't know what to say- he was asking for it." His voice was hard, confrontational.

"That's the problem Carter," I shook my head, looking back at Zach who was being helped out of the ambulance by the paramedic, "you think that it's not your fault."

"Was it?" He said it like a question, but I could tell by the twisted look on his face that he agreed with me.

"You threw the first punch."

Carter turned away from me, his hands clamped together on his lap, "you didn't hear what he was saying."

"Then tell me."

He paused. Then, "he was telling me that you weren't mine."

"Oh, Carter." I sighed, placing my right hand over clasped ones on his lap, "when are you going to realize that I'm not yours? I haven't been for a while."

The sound of a starting vehicle pulled us both out of the little bubble that we were in, our heads turning towards the retreating ambulance.

It was only then that I realized that it was getting dark and I had a shift at the library due to start anytime now, along with no way to get there. I bit down hard at my lip, turning my head to find Zach leaning patiently against the wall of the mall, his hands shoved into his pockets.

"I've got to go, Carter."

He nodded slowly, a calm façade falling over him. "I get it."

I stood then, the air around him felt dismissing- like he was done with not only the conversation, but he was done with me as well. Carter stood as well, walking away before I could open my mouth to say goodbye.

He hadn't always been like this. Carter used to be the boy who was cool, calm and collected- the one that never reacted no matter how much you pushed him.

Then his mother was diagnosed with cancer.

It was like a switch inside of him had been flipped and Carter had become a total different person. Her cancer had gone away a few years later, and the happy, carefree Carter had returned- the switch had been flipped back.

As I stood there, watching Carter walk away from me I had this funny feeling that the switch may have been reversed again.

I was chewing on my lip when Zach approached me, his hands still in his pockets. A hiss escaped my lips when I saw the black and purple bruise that already filled his face.

"And he doesn't even have a scratch on him." I said in awe, my fingers tracing the outline of a bruise on Zach's right cheek.

"I didn't want to fight back," he shrugged, cocking his head to the side, "is he okay?"

"He's fine." I wait a minute before saying, "I think he regrets what he did." I was paraphrasing but Zach didn't need to know that.

He nodded, accepting my answer- but I could tell by the glint in his eye that he didn't believe me. "Do you need a drive?"

"Are you okay to drive?"

Zach lifts up his hands, turning them over in front of me. "My face may not look so good but I don't need it to drive."

I laughed, before walking towards his car with him.

Carter wasn't the only man who could flip between two person-alities; Zach was exactly the same. There were moments that he was the kindest guy that I had ever met; like when I had first met him at the football game with Elli. Then Zach had these moments when he would turn into an egotistical jerk- the personality that was expected of him as the football captain.

I think that's why our relationship didn't work- because Zach could be such a jerk sometimes and I wasn't the type of girl to accept that. Yet the boy that I had first met was sweet and kind and that was the exact same boy that was talking to me right now.

"I can't believe you're actually working at a book store." Zach commented as he turned right down a street.

"Why?" I asked, a light undertone to my voice.

"I thought you hated books."

"I did- well, I do."

"Did or still do?"

"I don't know- I like some books, others I just, well, don't."

He nodded slowly, taking a left down another street that lead deeper into Toronto. He seemed hesitant to speak but quickly blurted out, "do you still love Carter?"

That was a question that had kept me up at night for months on end since Carter had re-entered my life. I had tried countless times to find an answer to it, but it was something that I still struggled with.

"I don't know." It was the truth, at least the best truth that I could come up with at the moment.

"What about me?"

The question caught me off guard, and I snapped my head to look at him in response. Did I still love Zach? Did I ever love Zach? "I don't know."

He nodded, accepting my answer as we pulled into the parking lot of the book store. "Would you go on another date with me?"

"What?" I breathed out, startled at the question.

He parked the car and turned to face me, grabbing both of my hands in his own. "Will you give me a second chance, Zoe?"

As I looked down at our connected hands and back up at the entrance of the book store, I wondered what my brother would think. The only message that I had been getting from Thea, Elli and my mum for months now was that I needed to take a step forward- move on. The book store hadn't done much for me like I had hoped. So maybe this was my chance.

I looked away from our hands and back at Zach, knowing that I would most likely regret my answer either way. Yet this was something that I had to do.

"Will you?" Zach prodded again, squeezing my hands as he spoke.

"Yes."

chapter 16

I used to think that I had life all figured out. I knew what clothes to wear to make other girls envious of me, I knew what colour to paint my lips to make the boys want to touch them with their own, and I knew what words to shove into an essay to make the teacher think that I knew exactly what they taught.

In reality, the only thing that I used to do was pretend. Pretend that I didn't hear the fights of my parent's rocking the walls of our house. Pretend that I didn't notice when Zach started cheating on me. Pretend that I was happy.

Now I was able to look back and realize that I wasn't happy, that I wasn't perfect. The little bubble of thinly veiled protection that I had built around myself had been shattered the minute my brother's car had crashed into little pieces- and I was left with nothing.

I was starting to realize that there was no such thing as perfect. I thought that my brother was right when he said that my relationship with Carter wasn't working because we weren't 'perfect' for each other. But in some ways we were- his loud and boisterous ways balanced out my quiet and calm personality. He was everything that I wasn't.

Yet, as I sat watching the snow fall around me, it wasn't hard for me to realize that we weren't the same people. His loud personality was gone; he was sullen, quiet- not the same popular boy that he was before. The same way that I had reverted even further back into my shell- fearing socialization the same way some people feared death.

We weren't the same; but he still got me. He knew what to say to get me to smile, he knew when I needed space, and- more importantly- he understood what I was going through. Carter didn't force me to move on like everyone else did, he didn't expect me to jump back into my old personality after one week. He knew. Although that didn't change that fact that he got behind the wheel drunk, with my brother by his side.

"You called?"

Elli. I looked up at the sound of her voice and gave her a small smile, Carter's face still at the forefront of my mind. God, even after I agree to go on a date with Zach I still can't stop thinking about him.

Elli walked across the park, her hands shoved deep into the pockets of her winter jacket and her cheeks tinged with a dull red from the battering blows of the wind. "Are you alright?" She asked, her eyebrows pulled together in the middle in obvious concern.

"No." I said softly, not meaning for her to hear hit- but by the way her face softens I can tell that she does.

Elli settled in next to me on the bench, sitting silently with me as we both watch the snow fall. It was only a few weeks until the holidays, nearly marking the conclusion of mine and Carter's work for our assignment. We're meant to present it only a few days before the break, and then Carter never has to talk to me again if he wishes. And, for some reason, the thought of never speaking to Carter again sends a pang through my chest.

"I heard what happened." Elli offered, her eyes still trained on the empty park in front of us. When I called her I didn't want her to come to my house; that would only start questions of where my dad was, so I volunteered the park at the end of the street. Although I regretted the decision the minute I stepped outside and saw the snow falling down- an event that was long overdue but was shocking nonetheless.

I pursed my lips in response to her comment, my mind drifting back to Zach's swollen face and Carter's overreaction. "It's been a while since I've seen him get that angry- since the first time his mum was diagnosed."

She nodded, her knees bouncing slightly as she made every effort to keep warm. "His mum's getting worse."

Although I was expecting it, the news still startled me. Carter's mother was a sweet lady, her brown hair always falling in loose waves, and it was only on rare occasions that I went over to his house and she wasn't baking. She was too sweet of a lady to have cancer. "But I thought she was in remission?"

"They think that it's come back, they're going in for secondary testing tomorrow." Elli shook her head, her eyes leaving mine to stare at a point far in the distance, her shoulders slumped slightly, "Carter's terrified that she won't make it."

My throat tightened, and I have to blink repeatedly to stop the tears from coming. Carter had always been the positive one, persistent that his mother wouldn't let cancer be the thing to stop her. So, to hear that he thought that there was a chance that this time may be the last is the worst thing for me to hear.

"They still don't know what stage she's at though," she quickly threw in, pulling her hands out of her pocket to blow into them, "so it could go either way."

"I should go see her." I said quickly, already planning the rest of my day in my head- if I went to Carter's house now I should be able to make it back in time for my mum not to notice that I got home a little later than I said I would be.

"Don't." Elli stopped me, placing her hand over mine, "today is their family day- the last day of not knowing." She pulled her hands back after that and placed them back into her coat pockets.

"Right," I settled back into the bench, feeling like a balloon that has just been popped, "of course." There was a time that I was a part of family days in Carter's household- so being reminded that I wasn't invited was still sometimes hard to hear.

"You'll see him at school tomorrow," Elli offered, obviously noticing my reaction, "and you can talk to him then."

"I don't think that we're exactly on talking terms." I said with a dry laugh, letting my head fall back so that I was staring up at the sky- watching the snowflakes fall right towards me.

Elli frowned, "since when?"

"Since Mark."

She let out a small breath at my response; obviously not happy with. Elli had always been our number one supporter, campaigning for our relationship years before we had finally gotten together. "Don't give me that crap, Zoe. You know that he was practically made for you."

"Oh, Elli- can't you tell that we're not the same people that we used to be. We just don't click anymore."

"Zo, if anything you're even more suited for each other now. You just need to talk to him-"

"I agreed to go on a date with Zach." I quickly cut her off, not wanting to hear anything else about Carter. It was difficult for me to hear about him when all I did was think about him.

"You idiot." She shook her head with a small laugh before standing up and leaving me alone on the bench. "I think that may have been the stupidest thing you've done in a while."

"Elli, please-"

She was already walking away as I spoke, raising her hand to cut me off, "Call me when you've cut that asshole out of your life." Then she turned around again, walking further and further into the thick wall of snow until she was gone.

My shoulder fell as I let out my breath- looking at the empty park before me, I couldn't help but feel more alone then I had before.

The walk to my house was short, only ten minutes. But it felt like I had been walking for hours when the sound of my ringing cellphone penetrated the silence around me. I reached into the pockets of my jacket, feeling around for the familiar metal of my phone. When I found it I pulled it and quickly pressed talk, hoping that it was Elli calling to apologize, "hello?"

"Zoe, honey? Is that you?"

Dad. I hadn't heard his voice in nearly a month, yet the minute the familiar rasp came down the line I couldn't help but feel like I had talked to him yesterday. "Dad?" My voice was high as my throat tightened, threatening my breath.

"Zoe!" He sounded happy- cheerful, better than he did when he was here. "I thought I had the wrong number when you didn't answer when I called."

"Dad." I said softly, not noticing that I had stopped walking only steps from the end of my driveway. "Where are you?" The sound of loud voices came down the line from behind him.

"Vegas." He said simply, his voice losing a couple of notches of his enthusiasm.

The news hit me like a punch to my stomach, my knees buckling under me until I was kneeling on the cold concrete of the sidewalk. "You left us to go to Vegas?"

"Honey, what's that? I can't really here you?" This time it was the sound of a girl laughter that followed his voice, along with the sound of him trying to quiet her. "I've got to go, I've got some business to attend to-"

"Dad-"

"Bye, Zo! Love you!"

Click.

I didn't know how long I was laying on the sidewalk, numb with the realization that my dad was done with us, until the sound of my mum's voice seemed to pull me from my trance.

"Zoe! Zoe, what happened?"

She was pulling me off of the snow filled ground before I had the chance to respond, pulling me into her arms. Her hands ran down my arms, over my hair, across my face as she tried so hard to fix me- not knowing what had broken me in the first place. "Are you okay, darling?"

As I nodded and wrapped my arms tightly around my mum, I couldn't help but wonder if one good thing may have come out of all the bad things that have happened lately.

CHAPTER 17

My mum used to tell me that sorry didn't mean anything. 'It's just a word,' she would scold me when I tried to brush things off with the apology.

I took her words with a grain of salt, tucking them away where I wouldn't access them for a while. So, I kept saying sorry- sorry to a person that I bumped into on the street, sorry to another driver when I cut them off, sorry to the cashier when I short-changed her. Sorry, sorry, sorry.

To me; it was nothing more than just a word- just as my mother had said. Used so often that it lost all meaning to me. It was reflexive, said as an excuse for my mistakes.

It wasn't until I first saw Carter after Mark's death did I realize what my mother truly meant. He was crying silent tears, lying lazily against his hospital bed when I walked in.

The first thing he said to me was that he was sorry. Instead of providing the comfort that Carter hoped it would, it felt more like a slap to the face. Sorry wouldn't right his wrong; sorry would never bring my brother back.

He was saying it to me now, sitting across from me at an empty table in the cafeteria save for the two of us. "I'm sorry for hurting

Zach," he said again, his face contorted in a way that I could only assume someone who was truly sorry would look.

Except he wasn't sorry. Hitting Zach was exactly what he wanted; if he were honestly sorry about it now, he wouldn't have done it in the first place.

"Then why did you do it?"

He let out a sigh, his eyes trailing away from me towards the empty tables that surrounded us. Carter had texted me the night before; insisting that we meet during fourth period- when no one else had lunch. I had to lie to my teacher to get out of class, something that caused my heart to pound and my hands to sweat- but I was beginning to think that it wasn't worth it. That maybe I would been better off sitting through my current class than sitting across from Carter.

"You know why I did it Zoe," his tone almost made me believe that I did know why he did it- I had to remind myself that I didn't. The excuse that he had given me in the mall parking lot was just that; an excuse.

"No," I shook my head slowly, trying to show him that I meant what I said, "I don't."

His eyebrows pulled together in the center, a look of pure confusion crossing his face. In Carter's book; he had a legitimate excuse for doing what he did, he saw what Zach said as provocation- I saw it as Zach stating the truth. "I don't know what else to say; I already told you why I did it."

"Oh, Carter," I resisted the urge to reach forward and grab his hand in my own as I spoke, "I don't know what else to say."

His frown receded as he appraised my calm demeanour; he knew that I meant what I said. I was done playing these games with him, if he wanted to act stupid and punch innocent people then I would no longer play the part of a bystander. He shrugged finally, seemingly puncturing the tension filled air around us, "then don't say anything."

That was his conclusion. He was done with me, done with the conversation. I was done with the topic of Zach as well, I knew that it wouldn't get us anywhere if we continued to talk about my ex-boyfriend. But I wasn't done with him- a blind person could see the ever growing bags under his eyes that could only be the result of one thing; his mother. "Is everything okay at home?" I asked, effectively changing the topic in the process.

He gave me his typical half grin, leaning back further into the plastic cafeteria seat, "of course," his grin faltered slightly as he spoke before it returned in full force. The only sign that something was wrong was the dullness of his eyes, like he was looking but not seeing that I was right in front of him.

I leaned forward, this time giving in and clasping his hand in mine, "you know that you can tell me anything, right? Just because we aren't together doesn't mean I don't care for you."

"I'm fine, Zoe." Carter pulled his hand away from mine, letting mine fall limp onto the table, "just let it go."

He wasn't fine. I could tell the minute that I laid eyes on him in the parking lot; he was sitting in the driver's seat of his car- his eyes closed and resting on the top of his steering wheel.

I hesitated on my way to my car, my grip on my car keys loosening as I stared in the opposite direction at Carter's car. People trailed around his car, weaving in and out as the all headed their respective ways- but none stopped to spare Carter even so much as a glance.

Gripping my car keys tighter in my hand, I turned away from my car and walked towards Carter- who still hadn't moved from his position. I walked around the front of his car, my feet slowly trudging through the freshly fallen snow until I was standing right in front of the driver's side car door. I raised my empty hand slowly, tapping on the window with the knuckles of my left hand.

He raised his head slowly, his eyes drifting towards my hand before trailing up my arm and landing on my face. Carter slowly closed his eyes, his head lulling against the head rest of his seat before he rolled down the window for me, "what do you want, Zoe?"

"Are you-"I stopped myself, remembering our earlier conversation, "okay?" I said finally, realizing that making sure that Carter was well was more important than resolving the existing tension from earlier.

He smiled; although it wasn't his regular warm smile, instead it was one that sent shivers down my spine- one that obviously didn't belong on his face, "what would make you think that I'm not?"

I pursed my lips, using the pressure from the action to stop myself from snapping at him, "Carter- now is not the time for games."

He rolled his eyes to look up at the sky, closing them briefly before turning his head back to look at me, "I've had a long day, Zoe- that's it; I'm fine."

I reached up a hand to grab the strap of my backpack, toying with the fraying edges. My eyes drifted towards the passenger seat. It felt wrong to leave Carter, when he obviously wasn't acting himself, but at the same time there was no way for me to place myself in that car next to him.

"Is that all?" His voice snapped me out of my thoughts, and as I watched the tired man in front of me reach forward to turn the key and start the car a creeping sense of panic overcame me- visions of Carter crashing his car played like a horrible movie on the back of my eyelids.

"We need to work on our project," I rushed the words out, my hand frantically reaching forward and clutching on to the rolled down window- like my weak hold would someone how stop him from leaving me behind.

"It's not due for a while," but I could tell by the softening look in his eyes that my frantic excuse had worked on him; if only enough to cause some doubt.

"Come on, we should really finish our last interview," I was already opening the back door and throwing my backpack on to the seat as I spoke, not taking a breath between words so as to prevent Carter from protesting.

As I opened the passenger door and waited for Carter to move his backpack so that I could sit, I slipped my car key into my jacket pocket- knowing that I had gotten into the right car after all.

We had been to the mall, we had been to a fancy restaurant- so, as Carter told me in an obvious tone, there was only one logical place left for us to go; McDonalds. Carter peeled into the fast-food restaurant's parking lot, flying over the skilfully placed speed bump before he cruised into a parking spot; coming to an abrupt stop.

"Well," I started, my shaking hand reaching down to unclip my seatbelt, "I think your driving ability may have regressed."

Carter pulled the key out of the ignition, letting out a frustrated sigh, "some of us have places to be, Zoe. We don't all have tons of free time."

"Of course," I hissed, already slamming the car door behind me before I stalked towards the McDonald's entrance, "let's get this over with then."

I could hear his heavy footsteps following close behind me. Thump. Thump. Thump. The repetitive sound reminded me of the ticking of the old clocks that hung above every classroom door at school. I liked to think that the loud sound was there to remind us that time was slipping away, and we were stuck in the confines of the classroom. Carter's footsteps behind me reminded me again that time was limited, and I couldn't help but wonder what we were counting down to now.

My hand rested on the metal door handle before I pulled it open quickly, letting it fall shut before Carter had the time to reach it. I could hear his cluck of disgust but his disapproving noises were drowned out the minute I stepped into the fast food place- the sound of screaming children and talking adults was much louder.

My gaze trailed over the patrons- looking for who couples that we could possibly interview, only there were none. As it was only a little after three o'clock, surrounding us were a bunch of young adults, teenagers, and children with their babysitters.

"I think we may have come to the wrong place," Carter pointed out, popping his lips when he finished talking.

I looked over the crowd again, my eyes narrowing in on a booth in a corner where a young mother sat, desperately trying to calm her crying child. I nodded my head towards where she sat before motioning for Carter to follow me- which he did with a small shrug, obviously wondering how we were going to talk to this girl about love when she was sitting alone.

We reached her just as the toddler closed her eyes, her loud screams coming to a halt. The mother looked visibly relieved at the silence that encompassed her after her daughter's tears halted.

I hesitated at the corner of the table, my fingers resting at the edge. The mother had collapsed with her head resting on the seat, and she looked so peaceful that I felt almost cruel interrupting her. Only I didn't have to be the person to capture her attention, because Carter reached forward and tapped her shoulder for me-effectively causing her to bolt upright and her child's tears to start again.

"Shit!" She cried, rocking her daughter back and forth in a pitiful attempt to get her back to sleep, "I just got her to sleep."

Carter rocked on the back of his heels, his emotionless expression telling the two of us that he truly did not care less. It was odd, to see him acting the way that most people expected him to- as the typical popular boy people normally thought that he was rude, cold, and being his friend an exclusive privilege; normally it wasn't. For most of us, it was easy to become his friend- but judging by the way that he was acting now, I could tell that approaching him in this mood would have him snapping your hand off.

"We're sorry," I said softly, watching the girl's tears come to an end as her whispered soothing things in her ears, "we were just wondering if you wouldn't mind answering a few questions."

She let out a laugh that was more sarcastic than true laughter before appraising Carter and eye with eyes outlined by heavy bags, "what do you kids want?"

Carter and I slipped into the bench across from her, both of us resting our hands on top of the table, "we just wanted to ask you about love, your experiences in love, and so on..." I trailed off, my eyes resting on her nearly sleeping daughter who had her head resting on her mother's arm.

"Oh God," she laughed that same non-laugh from before, her tired eyes drifting between the two of us, "could I go on about love- most stupid thing in the world in my opinion."

I nudged Carter, motioning for him to grab some paper and a pen out of his backpack. This, I couldn't help but think as I watched Carter do as I asked, is exactly what we need. We had the old lover, the young lovers- but we hadn't thought about incorporating the non-lovers; the people who didn't believe that love truly did exist.

We rattled off a few typical questions, learning that her name was Abigail and her daughter's name was Lauren- before we turned to our normal questions. It didn't take long before Carter and I silently agreed to just let Abigail, or Abby as she insisted we call her, talk- straying away from our unwritten script.

We were reaching the end of our interview when Abby said something that caught both Carter and I off guard- causing us both to just stop and listen, forgetting to write down what she was saying.

"He left me after he found out I was pregnant. Everyone around me told me to let him go, to forget about him- but let me tell you, it's not easy to forget the one that you love. He was everywhere, I'm not going to lie when I tell you that he still is. But I don't think I ever really loved him, I thought I did right up until the moment that my water broke," her eyes lowered to look at her daughter, now sleeping peacefully in her arms, "and then she was born- and my God, the moment that I first laid eyes on her I learned what love truly was. She's all that I think about now." Abby tucked a stray peace of Lauren's hair behind her ear before giving her a soft smile, "no matter how frustrated that I get with her, looking at Lauren like this- it makes it all worth it."

Abby and Lauren left shortly after that, leaving Carter and I sitting silently in the booth. He was finishing off some notes on what Abby had said and I was sitting with nothing but my own thoughts to keep me busy. I turned towards Carter, watching as he hunched over frame scribbled quickly on the lined piece of paper.

"Carter," I reached forward and placed my hand over his own, stopping his hurried writing, "are you sure that you're okay?" The question had been bothering me all night; it wasn't hard to notice him struggling to pay attention as his gaze trailed off so did his mind.

"Zoe," he drew out my name, his tone telling me that this was not a line that I wanted to cross.

"Carter, you can tell me anything."

His shoulders fell as a shaky breath escape him, his gaze turning away from me towards the customers around us. There were a few moments of silence before he turned his head to look back at me, "It's my mom, Zoe. She's getting worse."

I stilled, knowing that this was coming but hearing him conform it was like a slap to my face. I held Carter's gaze until silent tears escaped from his eyes, and then he was in my arms- letting me hold him as he cried, and then so did I. I cried for Carter, I cried for his mother, for my parents- and most of all I cried for myself. Sitting in the corner of McDonald's, Carter and I held each other until there were no more tears to shed.

CHAPTER 18

There was this eerie calm within the boundaries of the Fairview Cemetery. It always felt like the minute you crossed through the gates of the cemetery you entered into another world- a world where the bustling sounds that one would attribute to the streets of Toronto were replaced with the occasional crunching of leaves and quiet conversations of the people around you. It was almost like there was an unwritten contract saying that you must remain quiet while in the cemetery, when in fact there was no rule prohibiting it.

Yet my mother and I remained quiet, silently weaving our way in between the headstones lined in perfectly symmetrical rows. My brother's grave was tucked away in the back corner of the cemetery- my parent's had chosen it because the area surrounding it was rarely traveled, giving my brother the peace that he deserved.

My grip tightened around the flowers that I had in my hand as I laid my eyes on my brother's grave. The plastic wrap around the bouquet folded and groaned under my grip, reminding me not to hold the delicate flowers too tightly.

Together my mother and I stopped in front of his grave, both of us gazing down at the headstone. The silence surrounded us, now that the only things around us were trees and bushes- the other people left back at the entrance. At the time of my brother's death, I agreed that this was the perfect spot for his grave- somewhere that no one would see me cry. Nearly six months after he was first laid to rest, I couldn't help but think that this place was no longer suited for him. Mark was loud, outgoing, always the friendly face that you instinctively searched for in the crowd- and the silence surrounding his grave was another stark reminder that he was no longer here.

Mum kneeled in front of the headstone, her knees just brushing the edge of Mark's grave. She skimmed her hand over the engravings that depicted his name and our message for him, her actions mimicking how she would use to caress our hair when she tucked us into bed at night.

"Pass me the flowers, Zoe," she held out her hand towards me, her gaze barely flickered towards me before she was looking back at the headstone.

I did as she said, kneeling down next to her as she rested the bouquet on the front of his grave. I mimicked her earlier actions, brushing my hand against the rocky top of the headstone. We had been so shocked after his death that choosing what to inscribe on the front was a rushed decision, but looking at it now I couldn't help but reflect on just how fitting it really was;

Death leaves a heartache no one can heal, love leaves a memory no one can steal.

My thoughts drifted to Carter as I read the quote again, wondering if what it was saying was true for us. Maybe my relationship with Carter was nothing more than a memory that would never fade, that's why I felt so attached to him. It was possible that there was no pull between us, instead all that I felt was the lingering feelings associated with the memory of him.

Plus, despite what Elli had said, there was absolutely no chance of us developing a romantic relationship again. Not when I would spend every day watching him live his life when my brother was six feet under the very ground that I was standing on because of him.

The sun peaked through the cloud ridden sky, illuminating the area where we kneeled. Its heat hit me like a shove to my shoulders, pulling me out of my thoughts and back to the reality that I was living.

"Are you ready to go, darling?"

I looked to my mother, who stood now- her eyes watching a group of approaching people. Their voices got louder and louder as they got closer to us. "Whenever you are," I answered.

Mum reached down and tapped the headstone once more, her final goodbye. My mother was not the kind of person who talked out loud when she came to see Mark. She used to claim it was because she had little belief in the afterlife, but I knew it was because she didn't know what to say. There was only so many times that she could say sorry to him; even if everyone knew that it wasn't her fault.

I stood beside my mum just as the loud group passed us, their voices fading away as they did. "Do you think he's happy?"

Mum's shoulders deflated after I asked my question, her hand still resting lightly on the top of his headstone, "I'd like to think so."

I bit down on my bottom lip, using the pain to distract me from the persistent tears threatening to spill. Deep down, I didn't think that he was happy. He had goals, dreams, wishes- all things that he would never accomplish because his life was cut short. My brother wanted to go to university, become a lawyer, and have three kids. We all saw it happening too- I could see myself take on the persona of 'Auntie Zoe'; something that would never happen now. I didn't tell my mum this though, instead I just gave her a nod of my head and motioned for her to lead the way out of the cemetery.

"I feel guilty," the words slipped from my lips before my mum and I had the chance to clip our seatbelts into place. It was the nagging thought that had accompanied me since we first stepped foot in the cemetery- and it only intensified when I read the quote on my brother's grave.

"For what?" Her tone took on a hesitant one, like she knew that we were about to tread on to territory that we had both tried so hard to avoid.

I bit harder on my bottom lip, my eyebrows pulling together to form a frown. There were multiple things that I felt guilty for; my dad leaving, getting closer with Carter, but mostly I felt guilty because I finally felt ready to be happy.

Subconsciously in the weeks following Marks' death I made the decision to stop doing anything that made me happy. In my mind, since Mark would never be happy again then neither would I. I told my mum just that, explaining that I was finally ready to take a step forward but I couldn't help but feel like I didn't deserve it.

"Oh darling," her fingers drummed on the steering wheel as she took in what I said, "You know you're brother- he would have wanted you to be happy enough for the both of you."

I laughed at this because it was true. Mark was the type of guy who would have viewed the world in the total opposite way than myself- while I saw it as a reason for me to never smile again, Mark would have seen it as a chance for him to pass on his happiness to me.

"But that's not the only thing bothering you," she looked at me out of the corner of her eye as she drove us out of the cemetery.

It was true. There was still a small shred of guilt left nagging at me. And that piece of guilt had a face attached to it; Carter's. Even if my brother would want me to be happy; I don't think that he would agree with me falling in love with the person responsible for his death.

"I don't think Mark would like me getting this close to Carter."

Mum cocked her head to the side, even though she was facing the road I could tell that a look of pure confusion fell across her face, "your brother didn't want you two to date in the first place because he was jealous that you were getting so close to his best friend. I'm sure that he would be fine with it now, though."

This time it was me who was confused- didn't she get that I didn't want to have the hands of the man who killed my brother touching me? How did she not understand how guilty that thought only made me feel? "Mum, that's not why I don't want to be with Carter- I don't want to be with Carter because he- he killed Mark." The words hurt to say, but they were the truth that I had to face.

"Just because he didn't stop Mark from getting in the car doesn't mean that he was responsible for Mark's death, no one's to blame," she said it so matter of factually that it took a few seconds for what she was saying to fully sink in.

"Why should he have stopped Mark from getting in the car when he was the one driving?"

Mum shook her head, immediately pulling over to the side of the road so that she could turn to face me head on, "who told you that Carter was driving the car?"

I thought back, my mind spinning as I tried to grab a hold on a memory where my parent's flat out said that Carter was driving the car. I thought and thought, desperate to find it- but I came up empty, "The car was hit on the passenger side, then it slid into a telephone pole." Mark was on the passenger side. It was the only explanation that made sense.

"Oh, Zoe," she reached forward, pulling me towards her so that my head was resting limply on her chest, my hands hanging down by my sides, "Mark was driving, the car spun and hit the pole on the driver's side."

Mark is the only one to blame, the thought slapped me with the same force as a physical slap. I had been blaming Carter for something that he never did. He didn't get behind the wheel drunk- my brother did.

Carter didn't kill my brother.

CHAPTER 19

My mum barely had time to finish telling me the full story of what really happened before I insisted that she drove me to Carter's house. I knew that I needed to apologize; even though I could have gone the rest of my life without telling Carter what I really thought happened that night, the guilt from that alone would eat me alive.

We sat silently in the car, both of us consumed with our own thoughts. Carter didn't kill my brother, Carter wasn't drunk, Mark was driving. Carter didn't kill my brother, Carter wasn't drunk, Mark was driving.

The words repeated in my head like a mantra of truth; each time the hit me like a stab to the gut. I felt disgusted with myself, for not bothering to ask for the truth. But the truth had been so clear to me. So clean cut. I believed that there was no way that my brother could have been in the wrong, that my brother would have been stupid enough to get behind the wheel of the car drunk.

But he did.

Part of me was mad at my dad, for not explaining it to me further. Yet even broaching the topic of Mark's death would have sent our house into a small version of world war three. None of us wanted it to happen, so we swept it under the rug. I did it because I didn't want to think that Carter would do something to so dumb, and my parents did it because they couldn't believe that their son was to blame for his own death.

It only took moments for me to fly out of the car, practically throwing myself on to Carter's front door. I needed to apologize so badly that if it were to be the last thing that I ever did, I would be content.

Carter's mother, Adele, opened the front door. It took me a moment to realize that it was her. She was leaning against the front door with the majority of her body weight; like she couldn't bear to stand up on her own. Her hair was greasy, tied back into a loose bun and she looked like she had aged twenty years in what had been only a few months.

"Zoe," Adele's attempt of a smile came across as a grimace, like it took all of the energy she had to lift the corner of her lips up, "are you here to see Carter?"

I didn't have the chance to answer before the sound of heavy footsteps coming running down the stairs interrupted us, Carter materializing behind his mother moments later. "Mom, what are you doing out of bed?" His tone was filled with concern as he came over and wrapped his arm around her waist, giving me a fleeting smile before he lead her over to the stairs from which he had come.

"Come visit me soon, Zoe!" Adele called out as she disappeared up the stairs with Carter beside her, letting her lean against him.

I was only waiting for a few minutes before Carter came back, looking like a giant weight had been placed onto his shoulders. His eyes were half shut and his lips turned down in a frown. "What's up, Zoe?"

"I-"I stopped myself, realizing how stupid it would sound if I just said, well, for the past few months I thought that you killed my brother. So sorry about that by the way. I bit down on my lip before pointing towards the couch in the family room, "Do you mind if I have a seat?"

"Oh, right- of course." Carter motioned for me to come in, shutting the front door behind me.

I waited until we were sat on the couch across from each other, him looking at me with a confused glance and I doing everything in my power to not me make eye contact. Still struggling for a way to phrase my apology, I started with, "I'm sorry about your mother."

He shrugged, his shoulders falling so quickly I could almost see the weight on his shoulders weighing them down, "She has her bad days."

I nodded like I knew what he was talking about, when in reality I didn't. I could only imagine how hard it would be knowing that your mother is going to die. Not when per say, but knowing that it's coming- never knowing if it was going to be your last goodbye.

"Is that why you came?"

I shook my head, my eyes dancing between the pictures hanging on the walls- picture of Adele and her family long before she was first diagnosed, back when her hair wasn't a wig and she spent her Sunday's at the Pilates studio. I pulled my gaze away from the pictures and forced myself to look at Carter, meeting his concerned eyes served as another reminder of just how cruel I had been, "I wanted to apologize."

He cocked his head to the side, confusion flooding over his features. He doesn't know, the thought swirled around in my head, another stark reminder of how horrible I had been, Carter thinks

I was just mad for no reason. "For what?" He asked finally, his eyebrows still pulled together in a tight frown.

"There's no easy way to say this," I looked away from him again, knowing that the only way that I would be able to confess was if I wasn't forced to meet his kind gaze, "I, well- I never knew the full story of what happened the night of the crash, and-"

Carter shook his head, holding up his hand to stop me, "Zoe, it was my fault. No matter what anyone else says, I know that it was my fault," he said it was such passion that it was only then that I realized just how much Mark's death had affected him; no one had thought to tell him that it wasn't his fault- and as a result, he had lived the past six months with this horrible guilt.

"Carter stop-"

He continued to talk over me, voice raising in competition, "I should have stopped him from getting behind the wheel."

"Carter I thought you were driving," it came out as a yell, the ensuing moments were spent in an uncomfortable silence- the only sound was a clap like thunder as I instinctively raised my hand to cover my mouth. "That's why I've been so distant-"

"You thought I killed your brother?" He said it with such a painful tone that I couldn't help but cringe, turning away from him like he had slapped me. "Oh my God, Zoe-"he ran his hand down his face, tugging on his bottom lip like it was his only anchor to reality, "I thought you knew."

"My Dad just told me that there was a car accident and he was so mad at him for drinking and driving, I don't know, I just thought it meant you."

Carter rose from his spot on the couch, his feet shuffling across the vintage carpet on the floor as he came over to sit next to me- the couch dipping and pulling me into him. He wrapped his arm around my shoulder, tugging me even closer to him, "oh Zoe, I'm sorry no one told you."

That was Carter. I should have known that he would never be mad at me, he wouldn't hold something as simple as a miscommunication- mind you, a miscommunication that resulted in creating a large gap between us- cause him to get angry. Instead, he thought that it was me that needed comforting.

I let myself rest my head on his shoulder, revelling in the peace that the contact brought me. For once since Mark had passed away, I couldn't help but feel that there may just be a light at the end of the tunnel. It may require a bit more hiking to reach, but for the first time it felt possible; like it was no longer just a silly concept that I only read about in books. But until I reached the light, I was content right where I was.

Elli was waiting for me when I left Carter's house, she was sat on my mum's car- shivering beneath the thick lairs of her coat. A smile fell on her lips when she saw me walking down the driveway to meet her.

"Hey!" She let herself slide down the car until her feet met the asphalt, pushing herself off of the car with her hands, "how did it go?"

"Pretty good," I wrapped my arms loosely around her waist as a greeting. Elli hugged me tightly before letting go, motioning towards my mum's car.

"Your Mum called, she had to get to work so she asked me to make sure that you got home okay."

"I could've walked," but I was already grabbing the door handle to driver's side, tugging on it a couple of times to break through the frozen layer of snow that was covering it.

Elli shrugged, bundled up in the passenger seat, "she didn't know what kind of state you'd be in."

I pursed my lips in response, knowing that my mum thought that my conversation with Carter would only have a negative outcome. She always liked Carter as Mark's friend, but never as my boyfriend. Out of my family, my dad was the only one who seemed to like Carter no matter which role he was playing.

"So," Elli held out the word, a sneaky smirk coming on to her face, "how did you leave it?"

"What do you mean, how did we leave it?"

"I mean- are you guys lovers now? Or is there still that ridiculous sexual tension?"

I nearly veered us off the road as she spoke, shocked that she would be so blunt about something like that. There was no sexual tension between Carter and I, looking back I don't know if there ever was. "Don't be stupid, Elli."

"Come on," she stressed each word, "you've always loved Carter, and he's always loved you. It wouldn't be a surprise if you two started getting it on."

"Elli," I hissed like my mum was in the car, listening to our conversation, "I haven't been in love with him in years."

"Oh please," she rolled her eyes, turning in her seat to face me, "a blind person could see how much you two love each other."

"But I thought he killed my brother," I shook my head, keeping my eyes trained straight ahead so I didn't have to see the look on Elli's face. I know that my mum would have told her why I was over at Carter's, but for her to hear it from me would have been much different, "I convinced myself that I couldn't love him."

"So," I could tell by her tone that she didn't believe me, "just because you thought that you couldn't love him, doesn't mean that you actually don't love him."

I raised my eyes to look at the roof of the car before training my gaze back on the road, "I know that I don't love him, Elli- there's nothing there."

"What if," she shook her head like the thought made no sense to her, looking away out the car window at the quickly passing streets of Toronto, "what if you didn't actually love him before, but you love him now?"

The question spurred something up in, making reflect on how I felt when Carter and I were first in a relationship. It was the typical butterflies, little sparks when kissed; the fairy tale romance that I only ever read about in my mum's romance novels. But now Carter and I had fallen into this sense of comfort, like he knew what I was going to say before I did. He understood me in ways that no one else did. Was that love?

"But Zach..." I trailed off, knowing that Elli had me backed into a corner. Now my thoughts were only filled with Carter, Zach seemed like nothing but a distant memory.

"But Carter..." Elli mocked me, her own tone light and teasing- like she knew that I was already starting to feel backed into a corner.

As I pulled into Elli's driveway she handed me my phone, Zach's contact already opened. "Call him," Elli demanded, placing my phone in my hand, "and tell him that you've changed your mind."

While I watched Elli walk up her driveway, bouncing as she did, I pressed the call button- already knowing exactly what I was going to say to Zach. Even if I wasn't sure how I felt about Carter, that small tinge of doubt was enough to make me tell Zach that I couldn't go on a date with him.

Maybe I was in love with Carter, maybe I wasn't- either way, what Elli said played haunted me, repeating on an internal loop for the rest of the night.

CHAPTER 20

There was nothing said between Carter and I on what we would do now. We knew that we would move- in what direction we didn't know. It was possible that we would move backwards; regressing into a relationship that consisted of nothing more than stolen glances and nods of acknowledgment. A relationship like that was something that I probably deserved for treating Carter the way that I had.

Yet, on the other hand, there was moving forward. It was as if we were on a train, with each stop depicting the height of our relationship. The first stop, acquaintances. The second, friendship. The third, dating.

Sitting on this train was painful, neither Carter nor I knowing which stop the other would get off at. It would hurt if the next time that I saw Carter he barely even acknowledged me, but I knew that it was something that I probably deserved. Then, there was friendship. We had been there, done that- even have the shirt to prove it. But the last time we had slipped back in to being friends, ever conversation with him left a knot in my stomach. But at the same time I didn't know that I wanted to be dating Carter again.

We would be going to university in less than a year which would probably result in another painful breakup.

Sitting in my car, looking at the imposing façade of my school, it hit me just how much I didn't know what I which way I wanted my relationship with Carter to go.

So, I decided to let him do the talking. It would be up to him how he wanted to treat me. It was possible that after I left his house he realized what a horrible person I was, and that I wasn't the type of friend that he wanted in his life. But it was also possible that he thought that this was his chance to get back with me.

The internal battle of what I wanted now included what I wanted Carter to do, and there was no way that I was going to win.

I was struggling to come to a conclusion that wouldn't leave me with regrets, which only turned my stomach even more.

The sound of the first warning bell met my car, reminding me that I couldn't spend all day sulking within the confines of my vehicle. Reluctantly, I grabbed my backpack and locked my car, walking towards the doors of the last place that I wanted to be.

I was met with an eerie silence as I walked through the nearly empty hallways of the school; it was almost as if my peers knew the internal battle that was raging on inside of me and set the scenery to go with it.

"Zoe!"

The sound of Carter's voice echoed through the hallways, almost like it was chasing me as I walked away from him. Slowly I stopped moving, spinning on my heel to look at him. He looked tired, his hair standing up in all different directions like he had spent hours tugging on it. His face lit up when our eyes met, like he truly was happy to see me.

"Are you free?"

I frowned, free? "What do you mean?"

The bell rung, interrupting our exchange. Carter used that time to half-walk/half-jog towards me- a smile still spread across his lips, "tonight? Are you free?"

I thought about my Monday night, my plans for the night consisted of a tub of ice cream and some old cartoons. "Yes. Why?"

"Our project is almost due, would you like to work on it?" His hand shot out as he spoke, as if even being this close to me without touching me was an impossible task.

"Of course," I returned his soft smile, watching his hand as it briefly touched my cheek before falling back down to his side.

As I watched him walk away from me and go towards his class that he was no doubt late for, I knew that Carter had made his move. He had gotten on to the train that was going forward- but I still didn't know if I wanted to get on with him.

It was awkward. So incredibly, painfully awkward between Carter and I.

He sat on his bed and I sat across from him on the chair at his desk. Neither of us knew what to say, what topics wouldn't spark either a fight or, on the other hand, a reminder of what we had lost.

"Did you finish finding the text references?" I asked Carter, watching as his head popped up from one of the books that we had read in the class. I knew that the answer would be no, he was still furiously pawing through the pages in search of quotations that would work. But at that point I would have done anything to fill the painful silence between us.

"Not yet," slowly he looked back down to the pages in front of him, like he was a dog that had just been scolded by his owner.

"Would you like me to help you?" I hesitantly stood from my seated position, hovering between siting and standing.

"I can do it on my own." He said softly, his voice barely reaching my ears.

I sat back down in defeat, watching as he continued to flip through the pages of the book, skimming over what he had read hoping to find one that would tie in to the points that we had.

A frown pulled his eyebrows together, his eyes drifting off the pages of the book and up to meet mine. I could tell that something was bothering him. I hadn't known him for the majority of my life for me not to inherit that skill.

"What's wrong Carter?" I broached the topic carefully, knowing that his mother was still incredibly ill and her illness had taken up the majority of Carter's life.

"Nothing," he looked back down to the book, his gaze trailing across the pages absent-mindedly. It was almost as if he was looking but wasn't truly seeing.

As far as I knew Carter wouldn't hesitate to tell me what was wrong with his mother, not after I had seen her so sick last time. Plus, after our conversation the other night and the way that he had looked at me this morning I thought that we were past the tip toeing around each other stage. I was almost positive that we were back to where we were before.

"Carter..." I said it with a warning in my voice, trailing off at the end.

He continued to pay the book in his hands more attention than he did me, but I didn't let that stop me. Instead I continued to watch him.

I had done my work, finishing it in the past two hours that we had spent together. It was up to him to finish telling me the quotations so that we would be ready to present in the next week.

"Please, Carter."

He bit his lip in frustration, knowing that I wouldn't let this go, "Zoe, you're going to hate me."

I laughed, although it came out with little humour, "I thought we had left that water under the bridge."

"Zoe," Carter looked up at me with large eyes, like he wanted to take as much in as he possibly could, "I still love you."

It took a few moments for the words to seep in, when they did they hit me like I had run into a brick wall. "Carter," this time I said it with a pleading tone. I had taken all of the right steps forward, I was ready to move on. But this was not something that I was prepared for.

"Zoe, you're everything that I've ever wanted. I need you. I'm not me without you-"

"Carter, please." Tears came to my eyes as he continued to speak, his words repeatedly hitting me each time.

"I've never loved someone as much as I love you. I thought that I could do it without you, that I could move on, but I can't. I'm not the same person as I am with you."

I couldn't do this, not now. I wasn't ready to be such an anchor in someone's life when I could barely keep myself afloat.

"Carter, take me home."

So he did. The car ride was painful awkward; spent with me silently crying and Carter continuously shooting glances in my direction.

When we pulled up outside of my house I hopped out of the car before Carter could say anything to me, my feet slamming against the pavement as I tried desperately to make it to the front door before Carter could make it to me.

The sound of Carter calling out my name echoed behind me, but I ignored him- desperately shoving my key into the door. Looking back now, I wondered how I didn't notice the car sitting in my driveway. It should have been alarming when my mother wasn't supposed to be home right now.

I stumbled into the house, slamming the door shut behind me. I collapsed against the door moments later, realizing that I was safe. I was alone again.

"Zoe? Are you okay?"

My head snapped up at the sound of an all-to familiar voice calling my name, and what I saw was like a slap of realization.

There, standing in front of me, was my Dad.

CHAPTER 21

My dad had never been the spontaneous type. He was never the type of man who would randomly bring home flowers in hopes of brightening his wife's day, nor would he find the time during the week to remind his children how much they meant to him.

Instead he was very structural. My dad had a pattern, he would come home- play basketball when he had the time, or do his work instead. It was almost as though he penciled in us, his family, whenever he found the free time. In some ways it was insulting.

Yet, despite how strict he may have been in the past- seeing my dad standing in front of me was shocking. If he was going for the surprise factor, he had very much so achieved it.

"Dad?" The word barely slipped past my lips, like even my body couldn't believe that my dad was the one standing in front of me.

"Zoe!" He held his arms like he was a long lost uncle that had come home for a visit, not a father that was returning to his own home.

I took a small step back, nearly falling back into the front door as I did.

He couldn't be here.

He couldn't be here.

He couldn't-

"Where's your mum?" He rolled up on to his toes like I was hiding her behind me, his gaze drifting around the house that he had no doubt just been walking through- probably looking to see if we had replaced him like he had undoubtedly replaced us.

I bit down on my bottom lip to stop from telling him the truth; that my mum was on a date, moving on, starting over- however he wanted to view it.

The sound of a car pulling into our driveway saved me from answering. Although the little sense of relief that I felt quickly wiped away when I realized that must be my mum returning home, meaning that her new boyfriend was probably there with her.

I kept my back pressed against the front door as a slow smile spread across Dad's lips. "Is that her?" He started to walk closer to me, each step mimicking the pounding rhythm of my heartbeat. This man in front of me was not my dad, not the man that had taught me how to read, that had taught me how to love- that's why I couldn't let him see what was behind the door.

"You can't go out there," I let the words slip before I realized the repercussions that they would have. Immediately my dad knew that my mum wasn't just out; and judging by how quickly the smile fell from his face I could tell that he had a pretty good feeling of where she may have been.

"Let me through Zoe."

His hands were on my shoulders then, grabbing me and trying to pry me away from the door. I gripped the door handle like it was a lifesaver and my only tether to safety. Which, in that moment, I suppose that it was.

"Zoe." Now he grabbed me, one hand on my wrist and the other on my shoulder. As much as I was resisting, I was no match for my dad. I found myself sprawled across the floor in the proceeding moments, staring at the open door.

"What the hell are you doing here?"

The sound of my mother's voice had me pushing myself off of the carpet and following the trails that my dad had left through the imposing snow banks. I was met with the sight of my dad holding up my mother's date by his shirt collar and my mother attempting to pull my dad off.

"You need to let him go," my mum said, her hand resting just above my dad's back. Her voice was quieter this time, like she didn't want to cause a scene even though all of our neighbours were probably already peeking through their curtain windows.

My dad nodded, letting her date fall to the ground. It was odd to see my dad relent so easily, when normally he would let his rage get the better of him and he would never stop until he won. Both my mum and I were relieved though, and knew better than to question his sudden defeat.

"Of course, I'll do whatever you want," he paused for a moment, turning to look at my mum's date who was leaning against the car while he sat on the ground of our driveway, "after I do this." We didn't have a moment to stop him before he swung forward and hit my mum's poor date with a punch right between his eyes.

The silence that ensued was painful, as my dad shook off his hand and my mum simply stared at him with a raging look in her eyes.

"You need to leave," she spat each word out like she wanted the sentence to be branded across his skin.

"What's that?" My Dad leaned forward, taunting her.

"I thought that I would want you back," she took a step forward, her hand finger waving in front of his face, "but the truth is that I am done with you. You couldn't handle your own son's death, you even forgot that you had a daughter-"

"I didn't forget-"

"Shut up, and let me speak," she growled, stepping closer to him. My dad kept stepping away from her, edging closer and closer to the street, "I don't know what you think that you're doing but you need to get out of mine and my daughter's life, and don't you dare think about coming back."

"Please-"

"Go. Before I call the cops."

I don't know if I was relieved to see my father get in to his car and drive away. I suppose, looking back now, that I knew that man was not my father- in fact he was the furthest thing from the man that I had looked up to all of my life. Seeing him drive away was a small weight lifted off of my shoulders, because I knew that one of the poisons in our life was gone.

It felt like I was standing in a scene from one of those made for TV movies. My ex-boyfriend, looking lovelorn and broken standing across from me- me, frozen in the doorway of my classroom.

It wasn't like I had any right to be shocked, I knew that Carter was in my English class and had every right to be there. But, I just wasn't expecting him to be there looking at me like that.

Carter glanced away from me, his eyes drifting towards the board where, written in large block letters was:

PRESENTATIONS TODAY:

CARTER AND ZOE

AMY AND CAITLIN

I looked away from the board and back to Carter who had a small grimace on his face, like the thought of us having to socialize was paining him as much as it did me.

I gathered up the small ounce of courage that I had left, gripping my binder tightly in my hands and walking over to my desk.

"Zoe, I-"

I held up my hand as I slipped into my seat, placing my binder on the surface of my desk, "It's okay Carter. We just have to get through this one presentation and then you never have to speak to me again."

"That's not what I want Zoe, and you know it."

"Carter please-"

He shook his head, grabbing for my hand that was still hovering in the air, "I shouldn't have said what I did last night, I know that- but please don't cut me out again."

I let my eyelids flutter closed, the brief moment of rest seemed to invigorate me. Between my Dad returning last night and what Carter told me, it felt like my life was turning into nothing more than a cheap reality show.

"Alright class, take your seats!" I looked up as our teacher walked through the door, throwing his stuff down on to his desk before tapping on the board behind him, "Carter and Zoe, you're up first."

Carter grabbed the usb that contained our presentation on it and handed it to our teacher, allowing him to set it up on his computer. I collected our scripts from my binder and passed one to Carter, holding the other close to my chest.

"Alright," Carter smiled, setting his copy of the script down on to the desk so that he could clap his hands together before he turned to face the class, "our topic is love."

The presentation flew by smoothly, our class seemed to enjoy the presentation- which was a feat in high school when most people seemed to fall asleep whenever anyone but the teacher was talking.

Carter and I retreated to our desk to let Amy and Caitlin present next, both of us feeling like the wall that had been built between us had broken down. When we were both sat at our desks Carter hesitantly grabbed my hand, giving it a small squeeze that sent the smallest wave of sparks up my arm and through the rest of me before he let it fall. Perhaps this presentation was what we needed after all.

My mum had gone to bed early that night, claiming that she had to wake up early the next morning but I knew that in actuality she was just too exhausted from all that had happened in the past twenty-four hours. We both had felt it when the door that my dad had kept trying to push open had closed, and I think that we were both trying to figure out what to do now.

I climbed into my bed not long after my mother had climbed in to her own, knowing that all that my body wanted was sleep. Yet, as I closed my eyes all that I could see were images of Carter.

Carter and me at the beach.

Carter wrapping his arms around my waist as I stood at my locker.

Carter, me and my brother- all trying to beat each other in one of those silly racing video games.

Carter and I a thousand times over; smiling, laughing- happy.

I felt my hand reaching for my phone before I could even think otherwise, pressing his contact and holding it to my ear.

"Zoe? You do know it's like one in the morning right?"

"I can't lose you Carter." The words slipped out before I could hold them back, but I didn't regret them. They were the words that I had been holding back and I knew that I needed to say.

There was a pause for a moment, like he was taking in what I had said, "You won't Zoe."

"Promise?"

I heard him let out a heavy breath, like he had been holding it since I had first called, "I promise."

I paused for a moment, once again feeling as though I had no idea which direction our relationship was headed. But the only difference was that now, I knew that I wanted more from Carter. I needed him in my life, and if we were to just be friends it would always feel like something was missing.

"Can we take it slow?"

"What about Zach?" He spit his name out like it was venomous.

I laughed, my hands wrapping around the edge of my comforter and pulling it up to cover my shoulders, "I've already told him that I feel nothing for him, Carter."

"Good." It was almost like I could hear him smile on the other end of the line, "Then Zoe Finley, I will wait as long as you need."

CHAPTER 22

There was something special about the thought that some-one out there couldn't sleep because their thoughts were swarmed with only you, or that all they envisioned in their future was you and them together. Knowing that someone was in love with you was so much different than something like knowing that they had a crush on you. It was a feeling that I never wanted to loose.

I found myself walking on air during my Christmas vacation, dancing as my mum and I hung up the last decorations before Christmas began. I felt Carter's love carrying me as I walked around the house, adding that extra bounce to my step.

It didn't take much for my mum to notice that something had changed in my demeanour. In fact, a simple passerby would probably have been able to know that the way that I was acting was not normal for myself. Yet my mum didn't question it, instead she took that extra Christmas spirit and ran with it- playing Christmas music for us to dance too and taking holiday pictures whenever she could.

It almost as if I had stepped into a new world. One where it was just my mother and I, and one where a boy was in love with me.

And I was in love with the boy.

It was a realization that I had come to and one that I finally accepted when Carter had called me on New Year's Eve, just after lunch. My mum had disappeared to get ready for the night ahead and I had settled in, watching one of the many made for TV holiday movies that would stop playing in less than a week.

I had just settled under the blanket with the lights dimmed perfectly, when I heard my cell phone ring upstairs.

"Zo, aren't you going to get that?" Mum called down after it had rung a few times more.

"Just let it ring."

Her muffled voice cleared up as she came to stand at the top of the stairs, my ringing phone held in her hand, "are you sure? It's Carter on the phone."

There wasn't any other words that she could have said to have me crawling over the couch, the blankets trailing behind me, and practically throwing myself up the stairs to answer the phone.

"Hello?" I asked, breathless, as my mum walked away laughing in the background.

"Zo?"

"It's me." I answered, sliding down the wall to sit on the top step of the staircase, a goofy smile slipping on to my lips.

His voice came through with a tinge of sadness, not vindictive of a boy who was about to go out to a New Year's party, "what are you doing?"

"Right now?"

"Right now."

"I'm sitting on the stairs talking to you." I bit down hard on my lip after I spoke, knowing that something was off about Carter, "are you okay?"

"Now that I'm talking to you, I'm fine."

"Carter what happened?"

There was a pause. A pause so long that I had begun to wonder if the connection had fallen through when he finally spoke, "my mum's in the hospital. She wasn't feeling well, nothing serious- but I don't think that I can go out tonight."

"Then don't."

Carter let out a soft laugh that sounded more like a breath, "this is the first party that you've agreed to go to, I'm not going to take that away from you."

"Carter, shut up. I'll be over in a little bit."

"Zoe, I," he stopped talking for a moment, "I don't know what I would do without you."

"I'll see you soon, Carter."

I sat on the stairs for a few moments longer, my hand limply holding my phone as I waited for Carter's final words to settle in. It wasn't that I was shocked to hear him saying those words, it was that I was shocked to realize that I didn't know what I would do without him either.

In was in that moment that I realized that I was madly in love with the boy that loved me.

"Darling? Is everything alright?" Mum asked, standing behind me on the stairs. She had sweatpants and a sweater on, but her face was already filled with makeup. After the incident with my Dad she had been hesitant to go out on another date, but I had convinced her that it was New Year's- the perfect chance for a clean slate. So when she received the invitation to go on a date with a tall, dark and handsome (her words, not mine) man to a New Year's party- she snatched up the chance.

"Carter wants me to come over, so I think I'm going to head there now."

"Is he okay?" She asked, running her hands through my hair.

"It's his mum, although he made it sound like she would be alright." I leaned pack into her palm, still basking in the happiness from realizing that I was in love.

"I probably won't be here when you get back, and don't wait up either." She stilled her hand, resting it in a comforting manner, "are you sure that you're okay with this?"

"Mum, I think that we're both ready to be happy. You and Dad were always putting on a show, this is the furthest thing from it."

She knelt down so that she could place a kiss on my forehead, "you are wise beyond your years, beautiful girl." She stood back up, pulling me up by my hand so that I was standing with her, "I hope you're going to go tell that boy that you love him."

"Mum-"

"I'm sick of you two running in circles around each other. Now go," She pushed me lightly towards the stairs, "you two need each other."

As I settled in to my car, ready to make the small commute to Carter's house, I knew that my mum was right. I needed Carter like I never needed anyone before him.

In the same sense that my love for Carter had grown, so had my strength. I had officially healed, and I hadn't needed a job, or a distraction. Instead the key to my recovery was sitting in front of me all along.

I felt as though I was walking on air as I got out of my car and followed the pathway up to Carter's front door. It was like a light had been lit inside of me and all that I needed was Carter. He was the reason that I had a smile on my face, he was the reason that I felt like my brother was standing beside me today- he helped me find myself again.

My hand confidently knocked on the front door, resting there as I waited for the sound of Carter's footsteps.

The door opened and revealed Carter's dad, who looked like he had been dragged through hell and back, "Zoe?"

"Um, hi sir. I'm here to see Carter... Is he around?"

His dad pulled the door open wider, motioning upstairs, "He's in his room."

Slowly I stepped past him, resisting the urge to pull away like his grief and sadness was contagious. I started to walk up the stairs when I felt the need to turn around, "It'll get better- she'll get better."

He pursed his lips before giving me a small, sad smile, "I sure hope so, Zoe." With that he left the house with a duffel bag thrown over his shoulder.

I took a few moments to channel the happiness that I had felt earlier before I climbed the rest of the stairs and pushed open the door to Carter's room.

"You came," Carter beamed, looking up from the book that he had been reading.

I watched as his eyes reflected the happiness that I knew that he was feeling. My God was I in love with his eyes, and his smile, and every single thing about him. "I love you, Carter."

It only took seconds for his book to lay discarded at his feet and for him to be standing right in front of me. "What?"

"I love you."

His hands raised to hold my face, almost like he didn't think that I was real, "Say it again."

"I love you, Carter," I said it with tears in my eyes and a large smile spread across my lips. This was happiness. This was the joy that I had been looking for.

He wasted no time placing his lips on mine, and suddenly nothing else mattered but him and me. It was everything that I remembered yet at the same time something totally new. Carter and I had both grown up, but we were still the two silly kids who had fallen in love.

I thought that when Mark died that I would never be able to love again, but as Carter pulled my closer to him, smiling against my lips as we took a breath- I knew that was false. In fact, I had never fallen out of love.

It didn't take long before we had fallen to the ground and Carter's hands were roaming my body, trying to memorize every curve.

The way that he kissed me made it feel like he knew that we were at the climax, like everything else would be downhill from here. But as we kissed I couldn't help but feel like we were invincible.

"Answer it." I said softly after his phone had gone unanswered for the past ten minutes.

"But Zoe," Carter looked at me with tears in his eyes, still breathless. It was like he knew.

"-I love you Carter." I cut him off, holding out his phone for him to take, the phone flashing 'Dad'.

He nodded, taking a deep breath before pressing the talk button on his phone.

I waited in silence, watching as Carter's face fell and those tears that had formed in his eyes began to shed. We all saw it coming. Carter and I both knew that our moment had been too good to be true.

I held his hand, feeling his grip tighten the longer that the phone call went on, before the realization of what was being said came over him and Carter let the phone fall from his hand.

I wrapped my arms around his limp body, waiting for him to say something, anything. I knew then what it must have felt like for my friends when I was the empty shell that Carter had become.

"Oh Carter," I murmured, caressing his back and covering his face in small kisses, "talk to me."

"She's dead, Zoe." Carter broke down, burying his face into my shoulder, "my mum's dead."

CHAPTER 23

There is this sense of joy as the New Year comes, like a little voice is whispering to you and tell you that this year will be the one. This year will be the best yet.

This year will be filled with happiness.

I didn't feel that happiness though, not as I sat in the parking lot of the funeral home four days after New Year's. The snow was falling in a never ending wall that looked like it was barricading me in.

I drew a small picture in the fog of the window, a heart with 'C and Z' written in the middle before I quickly erased it. Carter hadn't called since I left him on New Year's Day in the arms of his dad, not that I expected him to. Instead it was his dad that had called to let us know that the funeral was today, and I quickly called Elli, who called everyone else to pass on the word.

My mum came back moments later, her cheeks tinged red and her mouth hidden behind her hands. She threw herself into the car, immediately putting her hands in front of the heater. "It's the right place," she confirmed. We both hadn't been in this part of Toronto before, so my mum wanted to make sure. "The service should begin in a few moments, are you ready to head up?"

I bit my lip before nodding. I knew that this wasn't going to be easy, but I also knew that I had to be there for Carter. I couldn't let him slip away from me like I slipped away from him.

Together my mum and I walked into the room where the service was being held and where they had just finished the visitation, Carter and his dad along with other family members were sat up at the front of the room. My breath stilled at the sight of his usually composed figure hunched over, his head in his hands as silent tears rocked his body.

Mum and I slipped into some empty seats next to Elli, who had surprisingly sat next to Maria. We each shared sad smiles, not knowing what to say. Death was a topic that was hard to approach when you were young, you were still at the point where your life had just begun.

The service was short, yet perfect. Carter's mum had always been the sweetest and kindest women that I knew, and the speeches that were given embodied her perfectly.

As people said their goodbyes to Carter and his family, Elli, Maria and I congregated in the back, my mum having gone home as Elli promised me a drive. We didn't want to go up with the rest of the crowd, but instead we decided to wait until we could get Carter alone.

A few other of our classmates gave us that same sad smile that we had shared as well as a shy wave as the left the funeral home, returning to the land where everything was okay for them.

I chewed on my nail as I watched Carter shrug off the few people that attempted to hug him or greet him in any way, knowing exactly how he must be feeling. I remember the numerous amounts of people telling me how they were so sorry for their loss, and they knew how I must feel. Their words hurt because they didn't know I felt, in fact I could only pray that they never felt this way.

Slowly the room emptied until it was only Carter and his family as well as us three left. I knew that it would be time for the burial soon, and that Carter would have to head up to the grave site- yet I couldn't let him leave without talking to him.

So Elli and I walked up to the front, leaving Maria behind, and watched as Carter turned around to us- his eyes bloodshot. He gave us a short glance before he turned back to his dad, mumbling hushed words. With one last glance in Elli and I's direction Carter slipped through a door at the front of the room, leaving us behind.

Elli and I stood frozen in the middle of the room, surrounded by empty chairs.

"He just needs some time," Carter's dad said, looking at us with a dazed look in his eyes like he was looking through us.

I nodded, knowing that could mean months or even years, yet I didn't want to broach the topic now- not when Carter's dad looked so broken. "I'm sorry for your loss."

He gave me a half-smile, "thanks, Zoe. Elli." With a nod to the both of us he disappeared through the same door that Carter had gone through.

"Well," Maria said from behind us, walking up the aisle to stand with us, "Carter looked like shit."

Carter did look like shit. He looked like he had the weight of the world on his shoulders and that nothing us really mattered besides the fact that his mum was dead.

"I can't lose him Elli, not again. Not when I just got him back." My voice cracked in the middle, tears threatening to spill over. The pain from having to sit through another funeral was intolerable, not when I could picture my brother is his casket and the speeches that my family had said. Yet for some reason, the thought of losing Carter hurt more than the thought of my brother's funeral.

"Now you know how we felt." Elli sighed, fiddling with the speaker controls of her car. We had already dropped of Maria at her house and we were now on our way to my house.

"I can't imagine-"I shook my head, stopping the thought. I never knew that my form of coping, cutting the rest of the world off, would hurt others that badly. Sitting here now I wondered how it must have felt for my friends to feel as though they had lost two friends and not just Mark.

"Let's just be grateful that we got you back." Elli gave me a smile, reaching over to squeeze my hand. Looking back, I would not have been able to picture myself sitting here, with Elli, now. I thought that my life and Elli's had permanently changed direc-tions, but it just goes to show how paths can always cross again.

"I just don't know what to do." I looked out the window, won-dering where Carter was right now. I know that after the funeral I went home and I cried into my pillow until there were no tears left.

"Yes you do, Zo. You always have. You understand that boy like other's only dream of. You know what he needs right now, not us. Just like he knew you when Mark died..." She trailed off, her gaze containing a mixture of both happiness and sadness as she thought about Mark, "You know, the day after the funeral we were all desperate to go to you, so that we could all be together, but Carter was persistent that you needed time. Yet as days dragged into weeks dragged into months we thought that we had lost you for good, but Carter knew. He's always loved you, that boy has."

"I've always loved him." I watched as Elli pulled into my drive-way, the light in the family room was on yet the rest of the house was dark. "I don't think that anything can change that."

"Then you know what to do." She reached over to give me shoulder a squeeze, "let me know what happens."

I gave her a quick hug before slipping out of her car to go into the house to join my mum. I felt myself dragging my feet, the weight of what had happened that day weighing heavily on my shoulders.

"You're home early." Mum looked up at me with a gaze filled with surprise, quickly moving to shuffle the papers that she had been writing on into one pile.

"What's that?" I asked, cocking my head towards the papers that she was trying to cover with her body.

"Oh, these?" Her voice raised slightly as she said like, like she knew exactly what I was talking about that.

"Those." They looked like official documents, and judging by the nice pen that my mum had dug out I knew that she thought so too.

"Well, you see..." Slowly she spread out the papers like they had been when I had come in, "I know that today isn't the best day for you to know this, not with everything that's going on but I'm filing for divorce."

CHAPTER 24

I hadn't felt like this in months, six months to be exact.

This feeling of fullness, like everything was okay. It was something that had been lacking in my life, yet I finally found it.

After staying up late talking with my mum about what the divorce meant for us and how we could finally take that step forward, I felt this same feeling come over me as I sat down on my bed. I was finally content.

My friends were back in my life, granted it wasn't the same relationship that we had before. I no longer hosted the parties and was viewed as the popular girl, but I still had my good true friends. It's true that nothing, not something materialistic like an iPhone or makeup, else matters when you have those friends. I had also found a new friendship with Maria. I think that she and Elli were finally getting along, so that didn't hurt my friendship dynamic either.

Then there was Thea. I had thought that after Mark's death she would resent me because I was a reminder of what she had lost. On the contrary I think that I was the reminder of Mark that she needed. Thea had even started coming over almost every other weekend to have dinner with my mother and I since we had started talking a few months ago.

It had taken me a while, but I had finally come to terms with the fact that Mark would be happy now. He would want me to move on. Mark was my best friend, he knew me better than I knew myself. I think that was why it was so hard to move on after his death. Not just because he was my brother, but because I didn't want to disappoint him. Although it had only taken a couple of different hands to pull me out of the hole that I had dug so that I could realize that my brother could never be disappointed in me. I was his sister, I was the first person that he turned to when he needed help. And I knew now that he would want me to be happy.

So, I made the decision that everything I did in the future, every choice that I made, was because I wanted to be happy. Not because someone else wanted me to do it, or because I was too afraid to step out of my comfort zone. No, I was going to do it for Mark, for my Dad, for everything and everyone that I had lost- yet everything that I had also gained. I knew that was what Mark would want, for me to live my life for me.

And Carter. My Carter. It had been a week that school had been back in sessions since Christmas break had ended, yet he still hadn't returned to school. I tried to call him but the minute that the connection would go through my call would be sent straight to voicemail. I knew what he was going through, and I knew that all he wanted was space. But I also knew Carter, like Elli said that I did. And I knew that if was allowed all that time by himself his thoughts would consume him and he'd dig himself down a whole that would be impossible to get out.

So yes, I did know Carter. And I knew that he was the exact opposite of me. Carter was the type of man that needed that attention, he needed someone to pull him back down when he got lost in his thoughts.

That was one of the many things that I loved about him, that he was the exact opposite of me. We contrasted each other in so many ways yet he continued to be the only person that truly understood me. And that was why I knew that I needed to go and see him.

"Have you tried texting him?" Ryder spoke up from the end of the table. We all had left school to go to a small little restaurant across the street for lunch.

I gave him a look that screamed 'duh', "of course I've tried to text him."

Ryder shrugged, picking at his plate of fries in front of him. I could tell by the slight red that spread across his cheeks that he was embarrassed, Ryder was never one to speak up in a group conversation. Yet I also knew that he was trying, trying for Carter and trying for me.

"I'm sorry, Ryder," I sighed, burying my face in my hands, "I just don't know what to do anymore."

"It's okay." He gave me a half smile when I lifted my face from my hands to meet his gaze, "we're all trying our best."

"Have you gone to his house yet?" Maria asked from her spot under John's arm. John was known for throwing parties and treating school like it was nothing, yet I could tell by the way that he continued to run his hand through Maria's hair that he might have found the girl to settle him down.

"Yes," I murmured, remembering the moment when Carter's dad had tried his hardest to convince me that he wasn't home yet I could hear Carter walking around the house in the background. "It didn't end so well."

"I say you go back and catch him off guard," Elli shrugged when she said, like she didn't want to be responsible if the plan didn't work.

I fiddled with my car keys, my burger and fries sitting untouched in front of me. The thought of Carter sitting alone in his room turned my stomach, since I knew how dangerous being locked away with your thoughts could be.

"Go." Elli whispered, the group distracted by the waitress who had come to check on us, "Make sure that he's alright. I'll tell the school that you weren't feeling well so you drove home or something."

I smiled, giving her hand a squeeze before quietly slipping out of my chair. "You're a gem, Elli."

I watched as all my friends gave me a wave goodbye as I left the restaurant before I hesitantly waved back. It was still new, the thought that my friends had stuck by me for this long. I knew that they didn't deserve the way that I had treated them yet I still couldn't help eternally grateful that they had all chosen to come back to me.

That was what friendship was. A choice. Unlike family, you get to choose who is and who is not your friend in this world. And that was why I knew that I owed everything that I had to those people, sitting at the table and still waving as I slipped into my car. They had chosen to come back for me, the same way that I was choosing to go to Carter.

The drive to his house was short, filled with me and my thoughts. I was concerned at what shape that I would find him in, but I knew that his father would never let him spiral so deep down that there was no hope left.

When I pulled into the driveway I saw Carter's blind peel open and a sliver of his bedroom light poke through before it closed shut again. Knowing that Carter was up in his bedroom sparked a burst of adrenaline through me, one that had me climbing up the steps to his house and banging on the front door.

"Carter! Let me in Carter! I know you're in there!" I continued banging for a few minutes before my fists pounded in rhythm with my tears. It hurt to know that he was sitting in his bedroom, ignoring me, especially when I knew that he needed me just as much as I needed him. "Carter, please..." My voice trailed off, and I quieted my pounding too, letting my head rest against his front door.

I listened to the quiet of the house, before I heard the sound of footsteps moving towards the door. I leaned back in time for Carter's Grandad to open the door, beaming down at me with his signature smile- although even he looked a little broken, which was understandable.

"He told me whatever I did not to let anyone in," he pulled the door open a little wider so that I could slip in to the house, "but do I ever listen? Nope!"

I laughed, tears still rolling down my face as I did. But at this point I was too grateful to finally be inside the house again that I didn't care how I looked.

"Zoe," he reached forward to grab my hand, squeezing it in his own, "I need you to help that boy."

I slowly nodded my head, knowing exactly what he meant, "I'll do everything that I can."

The stairs up to Carter's bedroom felt like they had been length- ened by a hundred miles yet I continued to walk them, each step feeling like I was getting closer and closer to the end.

I didn't know if that thought scared me or made me feel content. Maybe I was getting close to the end of our relationship, the end of Carter and I. Yet in the same sense it was also possible that

I was getting close to the end of the struggles. The end of the rollercoaster that had become my life.

With a shaky breath I pushed open the door to Carter's room, remembering two weeks earlier when all I had felt was joy but now all that I felt was dread.

At first glance it looked like there was no one in the room, the blinds were drawn and the lights were off, but when I looked closely I could see Carter curled in a ball next to his bed, "Oh, Carter..."

His body shook with a silent sob as I got closer, collapsing on to my knees so that I was kneeling next to him. With a shaky breath I ran my hand through his hair, watching as he pulled away an inch before he relented and moved so that he was resting his head on my lap. "Oh, Carter," I repeated over and over again, bending down to place kisses over his forehead before I collapsed into tears with him.

An hour later and we were both leaning against his bed, Carter still had his head rested in my lap but he had finally stretched out.

"Have I ever told you that I love you?" I began, breaking the silence. "Because I do. And my God Carter do I love everything about you, I love your hair, I love your eyes, I love your smile." I trailed my hand over his face as I spoke, touching each feature that I said, "but you can't do this to me ever again, Carter."

"I'm sorry, Zo." He reached up to grab my hand and rested or clasped hands next to his cheek.

"Don't be," I placed another kiss on his forehead, "you have no reason to be sorry." I waited a moment, my fingers absent mindedly running through his hair, "but you can't push me out like that again, Carter. I've just gotten you back and I can't lose you again."

He pushed himself up into a sitting position, wrapping his arms around me as he did, "I don't think that you'll ever be able to get rid of me, even if you tried." He hesitantly placed his lips on mine, like he still wasn't sure that he had any right to be getting this close to me. But I was more than okay with it, in fact, I would be content if I stayed in this moment for the rest of my life.

Because I had gotten my Carter back, and that was all that I need.

After Mark had died Carter had been able to recognize that I was the type of person that needed to heal on my own. I didn't need him, or any of my other friends bathing me in their love. I needed to figure it out myself. So he had given me time. He waited until I was ready to act as the director of my own; when I was finally ready to see that everything had gone wrong and call out take two.

And my God, will I always be grateful that the boy in my arms had waited. I don't think that I would have been able to make the final change had it not been for Carter, and I knew now that he was my other half. He was that person that stood behind me and held me up when I felt like I was about to fall, he was my tether to reality when it feels like everything is floating away; Carter Jacobs was my everything.

And I'll be damned if I ever let him go again.

EPILOGUE

D ad,

I knew that you wanted to be here today, to see me wearing the dress that has been sitting in my closet for months. But I understand why you didn't want to come.

Let me tell you Dad, I didn't expect that my life would be where it is now. Me, wearing one of the most gorgeous dresses that I had ever worn, about to walk down the aisle with Carter by my side. Needless to say, five years ago, sitting on the floor with an emotionally unstable Carter in my arms I could have never imagined that we would be where we were now.

But here we were. Carter was waiting for me downstairs, he told me that he wanted my appearance to be a surprise, but I knew that he was probably down there collecting his thoughts and prepping himself for the walk down the aisle.

With a deep breath I walked forward and hesitantly tapped on the adjoining door that lead to my mum's hotel room. I knew that she was probably more nervous than Carter. The last time that I had seen her she was sitting in her dress, hands shaking, as she waited for the clock to strike 1:00.

"Come in, darling."

I opened the door and found her in the exact position that I had left her, standing in front of the floor length mirror, smoothing her hands down her dress.

"Oh, my beautiful girl." Mum met my eyes in the mirror with a smile before she turned around. "You look stunning."

"Says the gorgeous bride." I reached forward to grab her shaking hand, "you're beautiful, Mum."

Jay and Mum are still doing well, even if it had taken him nearly four years to propose. We all knew from the way that they looked at each other when Mum had brought him home for the first time that it was only a matter of time before he proposed, although he did take his sweet time as I'm sure you agree.

"You think?" She turned around, facing the mirror once more. She smoothed her dress with her hands.

"Of course, Mum."

She let out a shaky laugh, obviously the nerves were getting the best of her.

Mum has been second guessing whether she should go through with the marriage again, not because she didn't know whether she was ready to spend the rest of her life with Jay, but because she didn't know if she was ready to move forward. This time the roles were reversed, I was the one pushing her telling her that I was ready and that Mark would approve.

The final push that she needed to start planning the wedding was the letter from you. After I called you I never expected for you to contact Mum directly, but now that you both are in better places I think that's what worked best. She didn't let me read the letter, although whatever you wrote had her in tears for hours after.

"Are you ready to go?" I asked the question as I gathered a few last minute thing from her room, holding the flowers in my hand before I motioned to the door.

With a shaky breath, my mum nodded her head. "I am, Zoe. I am."

She grabbed my hand and together we walked out of her hotel room and to the elevator.

She hadn't wanted a huge wedding like she had with you, but Jay's immediate family was too large to have the wedding in the backyard. So the wedding planner had suggested this hotel, it had a beautiful balcony that backed on to lake Ontario. Carter was waiting for us down in the lobby, Jay and my mum hadn't wanted a wedding party so we both had special seats for us in the front row. Although Jay is persistent that Mark would have been his best man, since whenever we tell him about Mark he says that Mark sounds like a man that would be his best friend.

"Am I doing the right thing?" Mum asked, turning to me as the elevator doors came to a close.

"Of course, this is the best thing that has happened to us in the past five years."

"But it won't be the only thing..." She trailed off, looking suggestively at my left hand that was bare of jewelry.

"I'm only twenty-two." I murmured, absent mindedly stroking my ring finger.

"And you two have been dating for five years, nearly six all together." Mum pointed out, taking her bouquet from my hands.

I rolled my eyes at her suggestion just as the elevator doors opened, revealing a nicely dressed Carter pacing a few feet away between the crowds who were about to descend on Toronto, "today's your day. Let's just get through today and then we'll talk."

Carter's eyes lit up as he saw my mum and I exit the elevator, his eyes sweeping up and down my body. Even I had to admit that I felt like I looked good in what I was wearing.

"You look beautiful," Carter reached forward to pull me into his arms, a goofy smile spreading across my face as he did. Five years later and he still made my heart race just as fast as the first time.

"Thank you." My mum said from behind me, a teasing smile on her face as she looked at the two of us, embracing in the middle of the hotel lobby.

"You look gorgeous as well." Carter complimented, letting me go so that his arm was only wrapped around my shoulder and I was standing against his side.

She laughed, "thank you, Carter. Although I do have to say that you two make a stunning couple."

I could feel a blush fall over my cheeks as I buried my face in Carter's shoulder, I still hadn't gotten used to the never ending compliments.

I suppose I had truly changed after Mark's death, I wasn't the same confident girl that I was before yet in some ways I was even more confident then I had ever been. I had become the person that I used to only dream of being.

Mum's wedding planner, Margaret, came rushing up to us. "Are you guys ready?"

"As I'll ever be." Mum said, the shakiness back in her voice.

Carter moved his arm so that it was wrapped around my waist instead, leading us towards the balcony entrance where the guests were seated and Jay was waiting on the other side. "Are you ready?"

I nodded, knowing that when Margaret opened the doors for Carter and I to walk down, followed by my mother, that there was only a fresh start on the other side.

Everything had finally fallen into place. All of my high school friends were seated in the audience, despite my mother wanting a small wedding, and Carter was by my side. Plus, the fact that you and Mum are on speaking terms helps immensely.

But most importantly I was in a better place, and I was happier then I had ever had been. I think that's because Mum and I have learned the beauty of stories, and how Mark hasn't truly left us, not when he is still with us every day in the stories that we tell. I hope that you're telling stories too, Dad.

"Well, Miss Finley," Carter motioned towards the opened doors and the aisle that laid before us, "it's time to take a trip down the aisle."

Love,

Zoe